SNOW SOCCER

SNOW SOCCER

DAVID TRIFUNOV

James Lorimer & Company Ltd., Publishers
Toronto

James Lorimer & Company Ltd., Publishers acknowledges the support of the Ontario Arts Council (OAC), an agency of the Government of Ontario, which in 2015-16 funded 1,676 individual artists and 1,125 organizations in 209 communities across Ontario for a total of $50.5 million. We acknowledge the support of the Canada Council for the Arts, which last year invested $153 million to bring the arts to Canadians throughout the country. This project has been made possible in part by the Government of Canada and with the support of the Ontario Media Development Corporation.

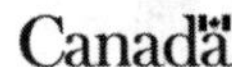

Cover design: Tyler Cleroux
Cover image: Shutterstock & iStock

Library and Archives Canada Cataloguing in Publication

Trifunov, David, author
Snow soccer / David Trifunov.

(Sports stories)
Issued in print and electronic formats.
ISBN 978-1-4594-1193-7 (paperback).--ISBN 978-1-4594-1195-1 (epub)

I. Title. II. Series: Sports stories (Toronto, Ont.)

PS8639.R535S66 2017 jC813'.6 C2016-906036-5
C2016-906037-3

Published by:
James Lorimer & Company Ltd., Publishers
117 Peter Street, Suite 304
Toronto, ON, Canada
M5V 0M3
www.lorimer.ca

Distributed by:
Formac Lorimer Books
5502 Atlantic Street
Halifax, NS, Canada
B3H 1G4

Printed and bound in Canada.
Manufactured by Friesens Corporation in Altona, Manitoba, Canada in January 2017.
Job #229617

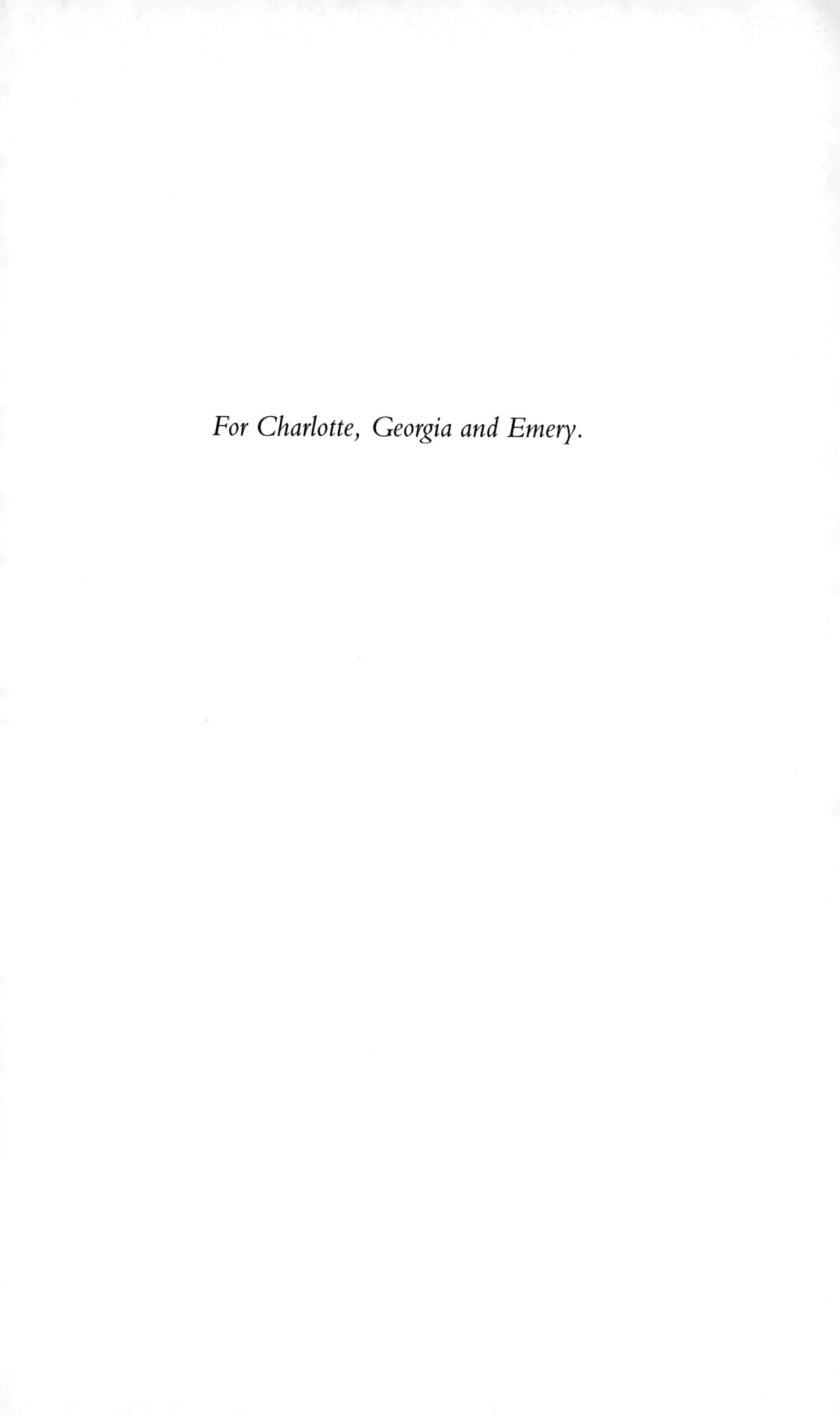

For Charlotte, Georgia and Emery.

Contents

1 BETWEEN TWO OLIVE TREES

Sarimah knew Hassan just well enough to feel sorry for him. She was planning to do something to him on the soccer field he would hate.

In every game they had played since his arrival at the Syrian refugee camp, Hassan had tried a slide tackle. Sometimes he got the ball. Sometimes he blocked a shot. Sometimes he knocked someone — usually Sarimah — to the ground.

Now, Sarimah had a plan. She found herself on the right wing with plenty of space leading to the goal. Hassan was playing centre defence and turned to chase her.

"Here I come, Sarimah!" he shouted.

Sarimah smiled and took two long strides down the wing. She could see Hassan start to slide. She dug her toe into the soft sand under the ball. She flicked the ball high into the air with her foot. Hassan could only watch as it arched above his head.

Sarimah stopped suddenly and Hassan skidded

past her. *Whoosh*. He slid through the sandy field, out of bounds.

Sarimah caught up to the ball down the empty wing. The goaltender, Aamir, was alone. Sarimah faked a shot with her right foot to put Aamir on the ground in a dive. She cut hard to the left with the ball and kicked home the winning goal with her left foot.

"Gooooaaalll!" shouted Hamza, who was on Sarimah's team. "We win! We win!"

Sarimah and the other kids gathered near the net to celebrate or console each other.

Sarimah glanced back over her shoulder. Hassan was marching toward them.

"Where did you find that move?" he said. "You have never done anything like that before."

He dusted himself off, shaking sand from his hair. Sarimah had learned it was better to let him cool down on his own. She found a water bottle and then plunked herself down in the shade.

"Hassan," she said, finally. "It took you a long time to walk all the way down the field from where you were."

"Oooh," Hamza said, "that was funny!"

"I bet you couldn't even see my goal from where you were," Sarimah, now smiling widely, continued.

Hassan raised his finger to speak. But no sound came from his mouth.

There were more snickers.

"I mean, I don't blame you," she said, trying to hold back her laughter. "You looked comfortable there, down on the ground."

"Ah, she's done it again," Aamir said with a grin.

"I must have hit a hole in the field," Hassan said. "I tripped and fell. It was unfair of you to take advantage of my injury."

"Hee hee!" Hamza was laughing so hard it was all anyone could hear.

Sarimah stood up and put a hand on Hassan's shoulder. She thought maybe he really was hurt.

"Hassan, that is awful. I feel bad."

"Thank you, Sarimah. I was hoping some of you were going to check on me. But it is okay. I am fine, really."

Sarimah knew he was upset. Even though Hassan was a rough player, he and Sarimah were friends. She started to feel bad.

"No, I am serious," she said. "We came to this camp about the same time. Every day we watch for your mother and sister to come. I need you to be in good shape for them. I can't start kicking you around on the soccer field."

She stopped talking suddenly. She realized she shouldn't be reminding Hassan of his family. He had made the trip to the Turkish camp with about seventy-five others from his village. But his mother had stayed behind to look after his sick younger sister and his grandmother. She had promised they would be right behind him. That was a year ago.

Sarimah guessed it was why Hassan got so angry playing soccer. Off the field he was much nicer. He looked at her and cracked a smile.

"Okay," he said. He went to retrieve the ball from behind two olive trees. "We will have a penalty shoot-out to decide the real winner. Aamir, you're in goal. We each get one shot. Hamza is first."

Sarimah liked the idea. She counted twelve yards from the goal to mark the penalty spot.

Hamza shrugged his shoulders. He grabbed the ball — a gift from an aid worker a year ago — and tried to bounce it. They had patched and repaired it so often, it hardly moved once it hit the ground.

Hamza placed it on the spot. Then he took ten steps back and studied the goal.

"Oh, hurry already. The fighting back home is going to be finished by the time you shoot," Hassan shouted.

Hamza began his run and tried blasting a shot up the middle. It went straight into Aamir's belly. He caught it with a satisfying *thud*.

"Ha! Nice try! Who is next?" called Aamir.

Hassan stood at the penalty spot. He put the ball down. Then he picked it up and replaced it again two more times. Each time it rolled a little, he put it back in a different place.

Aamir pretended to fall asleep: "*Zzzz.*"

Finally, Hassan took two steps back and then sprinted forward. He hit the ball confidently, but it sailed wide to the left. "Nah!" he said in disgust, as a couple of Turkish camp workers went after the ball.

"That's two!" Aamir said. "Let's go, Sarimah."

The camp workers threw the ball back to Sarimah and stopped to watch. Some of the other refugees had heard the laughing and decided to watch, too.

"Okay," Aamir said. "If she scores, Sarimah is world champion."

Sarimah put the ball down and stepped way back. She glanced at the bottom right corner of the goal before starting her run. Instead of shooting there, though, she hit the ball hard to the left. Aamir was already diving the wrong way and Sarimah scored with ease.

"Gooaall!" Hamza shouted.

Sarimah lifted her hands in the air and heard what sounded like cheering.

"Sarimah! Sarimah!"

She turned to see her father rushing toward her from across the field. He had never told her to stop playing football with boys before, but she was suddenly worried.

"Papa," said Sarimah, "what are you doing here?"

"Come quickly," her father said. He grabbed her hand and led her away.

"Where are you taking me?"

"Canada."

2 SPONSORSHIP TEAM

As flight 1121 from Toronto banked slightly to come in for the landing, Sarimah pressed her forehead against the window. Was there anything to see on the ground? Her ears popped and the airplane began to turn toward Saskatoon International Airport. She could suddenly see everything, but the ground was still flat. Sarimah thought it looked like someone had drawn the roads on the ground with a ruler. The highways stretched on forever in straight lines.

"Papa, where are the hills? Or the oceans?" she asked her father in Arabic.

He leaned over Sarimah's mother, who was sitting between them in the middle seat. He peered out the window.

"We are in farmland," he said. "Flat, so you can plant many crops. This is a wonderful place to live. There is so much here. We are lucky."

Sarimah looked back down to the ground again. She thought it would have been lucky to see at least a mountain or a beach.

She kept staring out the window. She watched the ground speed under her until the airplane bounced slightly and rushed to a stop.

Here we are, she thought. *Our new home.*

Sarimah and her parents were the last passengers to leave the airplane. A flight attendant motioned for them to stay. Then he had them follow him into the terminal.

"Welcome to Saskatoon," he said.

He was not the last person to welcome them. More people smiled politely and greeted them. A woman who worked for the airline gave Sarimah a bag of candy. Sarimah eagerly opened and devoured about half the candy as her parents signed forms and shook hands with other adults.

Finally, after Sarimah's parents had all their paperwork approved, a smiling airport worker motioned for them to follow him. He led them through sliding double-doors to where a crowd of people cheered. Sarimah looked around. Was there someone famous coming in behind them? But, no, everyone was watching Sarimah and her parents. Cameras flashed and someone started singing in Arabic. Sarimah realized that the group of about a dozen people was cheering for her family. She grabbed her mother around the waist and tried to hide.

A man walked up to her father and extended his hand.

"*As-Salaam-Alaikum,*" the man said.

Her father replied, "*Wa-Alaikum-Salaam.*"

The translator said his name was Mohammed and introduced them to the group.

"These are your sponsors," he told Sarimah and her parents. "They worked hard to bring you here. They will help you learn about Canada."

Sarimah looked at the people more closely. She saw an older man and his wife dabbing tears from their eyes. Another older couple was smiling and laughing as they waved at Sarimah. Three more women stood off to the side without saying much. An older man was singing and dancing. He was holding a sign that said, in Arabic, "Welcome."

Mohammed spent a few minutes speaking to the adults before turning to Sarimah.

"Everyone calls me *Mo*," he said. "Your father says you speak good English."

A scrunched-up smile spread across Sarimah's face. She had to think of her answer before saying it. She was also trying to understand why anyone would call a man named Mohammed *Mo*.

"I am not that good," she said.

"Good enough," Mo said with a smile. He turned back to the sponsors. "Sarimah speaks some English," he explained to them. "Some Syrian children — those in the big cities, anyway — studied English before the war. She will be a quick learner, from what her father tells me."

Sarimah noticed that hidden in the middle of the group was a younger family. The man and woman looked about the same age as her parents. They stepped aside and a young girl walked forward.

Mo stepped beside Sarimah.

"This is Isobel. *Izzy*," he said. "Her family owns the place you will be living at. You will be neighbours. She can also help you at school."

"Call me Izzy," said the girl, who looked the same age as Sarimah.

Sarimah could feel her face wrinkle again.

"Hello, *Izz-he*," she said, slowly.

Mo laughed and the girls turned to him.

"I think she is having trouble with our nicknames," Mo said. "Sarimah, Canadians love to use nicknames. It is a sign of friendship. You will get the hang of them."

Izzy handed Sarimah a paper shopping bag. Sarimah peeked inside. There were two T-shirts, some socks, a pair of pants and a sweater. She reached into the bag and shuffled the contents around. There were more things in the bottom: a toothbrush, toothpaste, lip balm, hand cream, a brush and hair elastics.

"Thank you," she said in English.

"I hope they fit," Izzy said. "If you want to return them, the receipt is in the bag."

The girls stood for a while not saying anything. The adults started to talk again, so Sarimah slid to the side, out of the way. She watched as Izzy did the same.

After what seemed like hours to Sarimah, they piled into a grey minivan and started the drive home. Sarimah sat in the third row next to Izzy. Sarimah sat on the right side and Izzy was on the left. The middle seat was empty. Sarimah's parents were in the middle row with Mo.

Sarimah tried to follow along as Mo described what they were seeing out the window. But it was dark and she was tired. She had a hard time keeping her eyes open and didn't see much until they arrived at their new home. Everyone piled out of the car and Izzy motioned to Sarimah to follow. Izzy took her around back, where a door led to the place Sarimah and her parents would live.

Sarimah walked through the door, up a short flight of stairs and into their new home. It was small, but clean and bright. A vase on the kitchen table held fresh flowers. Izzy opened the refrigerator door to show shelves stuffed with food. Sarimah stepped beside her and felt her eyes widen.

She spotted milk, and the vegetable drawers were crammed full of carrots, greens and red peppers. After that, though, she didn't know what all the bottles and cans contained. Everything was so bright, especially a cake topped with orange icing and a picture of a smiling, cartoon rabbit eating a carrot. Sarimah wondered what if it was carrots or rabbits inside. She hoped it was carrots.

The two girls walked down a hall to Sarimah's room. It had a bed and small desk. There was with a TV on top of a dresser. Sarimah saw there were already some books on a shelf by the window and a radio and lamp on a bedside table. Izzy picked up the remote control and clicked on the TV.

It came to life on a sports channel showing a soccer game.

"Ah!" Sarimah said, pointing at the screen.

Izzy looked at her. "You like soccer?"

"Football," Sarimah said. "Yes. I like it. I play."

She sat down on the edge of the bed. Her eyes never left the screen. Izzy smiled, sat down beside her, and turned up the volume.

"I think we're going to be friends," Izzy said.

"This team is the Whitecaps," Izzy said. "They're from Vancouver. They're playing the L.A. Galaxy."

"David Beckham," Sarimah said.

"Yeah, but he's not playing anymore. Is he your favourite player?"

"No, I like Messi."

Izzy jumped up from the bed. She skipped around Sarimah and ran into the hallway. Sarimah could hear her put on her shoes and leave the apartment. Her parents, Izzy's parents and Mo were talking in the kitchen.

"Izzy, where are you going?" her mother asked.

"Be right back."

Sarimah smiled. She was confused, but she could watch the game. Within a few minutes, she heard the door open again. Sarimah could hear Izzy taking off her shoes and running back down the hallway.

Izzy was now wearing a blue-and-white striped soccer jersey. She carried a poster. She put some thumb-tacks down on the dresser and unrolled the poster to show Sarimah. It said 'Lionel Messi' across the top and 'Argentina' along the bottom.

"This is for your room," she said.

She held one corner and Sarimah stood up to grab a tack. They hung it on the wall and then stood back to see if it was straight.

"Perfect," Izzy said. "Everyone at school likes either Messi or Cristiano Ronaldo."

"Your school," Sarimah said, "do you like it?"

"Oh, yeah, it's pretty good," Izzy said. "We have some fun. It's already November, so it might start snowing any day. That isn't as much fun."

"How much snow?"

"Probably a lot more than you're used to. At least we can play snow soccer then."

"Snow soccer?" It was two words that Sarimah knew. But the idea of soccer and snow weren't making much sense together in her head. Was she tired from the trip?

"It's great training for indoor soccer," Izzy said.

Sarimah looked up at the TV as the announcers raised their voices. The player on TV missed the shot, so Sarimah looked back at Izzy. “Don’t you play soccer outside on the grass?”

Izzy began laughing. “Oh, yeah, but it’s cold for a long time here. We have to play whenever and wherever we can.”

Sarimah looked at Izzy and smiled. That, she could understand. She decided Canada wasn’t so scary after all.

3 CLASS PRESENTATION

Sarimah and Izzy stood up from their desks together. They walked to the front of the Grade 7 social studies class at Thornton Park School.

As she walked up the aisle, Sarimah glanced out the window. She noticed that grey clouds had blanketed the city since the morning. *The snow can't be far off,* she thought.

Arriving at the front of the class, she was proud she could read the words on the whiteboard: "Saskatoon and Syrian refugees group presentations."

Sarimah glanced down at the notes and newspaper clippings in her hands. One was from the day she had arrived in Saskatoon: Friday, October 1. Exactly one month had passed.

"When I met Sarimah at the airport, she was very shy and didn't say much," Izzy started. "Since then, we have become neighbours, classmates and friends. Her English is so good. She has worked very hard."

Sarimah lifted a piece of paper and began reading

her part. “I arrived from a refugee camp in Turkey with help from sponsors like Izzy and her family.” She concentrated on every word. “I was scared at first. Everything was different here. But Izzy helped me.”

They continued to take turns for about five minutes. Sarimah told the class that she had learned Izzy was born in Ottawa, but moved to Saskatoon when she was three years old. Izzy told the class Sarimah was born in Aleppo, a city of two million people, before the war.

“Aleppo is one of the oldest cities in the world,” Izzy said. “It is now almost all ruined because of the war. Sarimah and her family may never get to see their home again. They told refugee camp workers they would like to live somewhere peaceful. The workers suggested Canada.”

Sarimah paused as a lump in her throat started to burn. “Syrian people are peaceful,” she said, her eyes starting to fill with tears. She blinked and they ran down her cheeks. The teacher walked over to Sarimah with a box of tissues. Sarimah took one and dried her eyes. She cleared her throat.

“I’m sorry. We saw some awful things as we escaped,” she said. “But I hope you get to see my beautiful city one day. I hope the fighting stops and you can see that Syria is more than just war.”

Sarimah looked at Izzy, whose chin was shaking. Even their teacher was holding a tissue close. A little embarrassed by her tears, Sarimah raised her eyes to see her classmates. Most of them were leaning forward, listening closely as Sarimah talked about how the Syrian war had created the most refugees since World War II.

Then someone laughed. It was a quiet giggle and whoever did it tried to make it stop.

Sarimah spotted her classmates, Tamsen and Kaelynn, in the back row. They were leaning across the aisle and whispering to each other. The teacher noticed them, too.

"Tammy and Kaelynn, I really hope you're not talking about your soccer team," the teacher said. "You can talk all you want during lunch-hour detention."

The whole class turned to look at the two girls. Sarimah was a little hurt. Their laughter had made her sadness seem silly. But if they were talking about soccer, she wanted to know more. She also wanted a blue-and-orange jacket like the one they both wore every day. It had a 'Blizzard' logo on the front. Sarimah knew Izzy had one, also, but didn't wear it as much as Tamsen.

Tamsen groaned and Kaelynn huffed. Sarimah could sense tension as everyone waited for their talk to continue. Finally, Izzy said they were finished. Sarimah was grateful to hear the school bell ring for recess.

Sarimah and Izzy waited for everyone to leave before they returned to their desks to collect their books.

"You are doing so well," Sarimah's teacher said as they left. "Your English is improving all the time. Just keep practising."

Sarimah and Izzy headed into the hallway to their shared locker. They were still wiping tears from their eyes as they arrived. But Sarimah was happy to have their talk finished. She put on her jacket.

"Hey, neighbour," Izzy said. "It's pretty chilly outside. Hope you brought your hat and mitts. You ready for the snow?"

Sarimah reached down and put her hand into the pocket of her winter coat. She pulled out a white toque with a green husky dog on it. From the left pocket, she produced her gloves and slipped them onto her hands. They headed for the double doors at the back of the school.

"Yes, I can't wait," Sarimah said. "But what do you mean, 'pretty chilly'?"

Izzy pushed open the doors and a blast of icy wind hit them.

"That's 'pretty chilly'."

"I see. I would say it is cold. Let's run," Sarimah said. "I might freeze like an ice-man."

Izzy started to laugh. "Snowman! Ah, never mind. I know what you mean."

"I have one thing to ask you, Izzy," said Sarimah. "Why did those girls laugh? Were they really whispering about soccer?"

Izzy rolled her eyes. "Oh, probably," she said. "That's all Tammy can think about. She's already talking about what college she's going to pick. She says she wants to make the Olympic team before she's twenty."

Sarimah had never met anyone who hoped to play soccer at that level. She didn't know someone so good went to Thornton. She felt proud of being Tamsen's classmate. "Wow! That is amazing."

"Just don't believe it. Tammy is good, but she's not that good. At least, she isn't yet. Maybe she'll make Team Canada, but right now I'm not even sure she's the best on our team."

Sarimah was confused now. She couldn't understand why anyone would make up stories about playing in the Olympics.

"I would like to see her play."

"Well, you can. She's right there. C'mon, let's go see for ourselves."

Izzy pointed over Sarimah's shoulder to the soccer fields. "Let's play?"

There was a group of eight kids chasing a ball.

"Yes, I guess so," Sarimah said.

She wasn't sure about playing with others after what had happened in class. But she really wanted to play. Sarimah and Izzy jogged over to the soccer field.

"Hey, listen up," Izzy said. "Sarimah is finished with her English classes at recess. She's free from the teachers!"

"Just don't put her on my team," said one voice.

Sarimah's heart sank. She wanted to run back into the school. She recognized the voice as Tamsen's. And she could tell that Tamsen was angry.

4 WHAT BRINGS YOU HERE?

"*Ohhhh-kay*," Brandt said. He was in Sarimah's class. She could tell from his voice that the tension she had felt in the classroom had spilled outside.

"You two can be on our team," Brandt said to Sarimah and Izzy. "We are going that way." He pointed with a mittened hand.

Izzy and Sarimah moved over to their team's side.

"Hey, Tammy, isn't your knee sore?" Brandt asked. "Are you sure you want to play?"

Tamsen was holding the ball. She juggled it a few times on one foot and then booted it toward Brandt. It landed right at his feet.

"Yeah, my knee is fine," she said. "Even if it's a bit sore, I'm still better than anyone out here."

Sarimah felt that Tamsen was talking about her. She did her best to ignore it. She didn't care if Tamsen got into trouble during her talk in class. Sarimah had arrived in Canada a month ago. For most of that time, she had studied English at recess while everyone else ran around outside. But Sarimah was ready to have fun, finally. She bounced on her toes as the two teams divided the small field in half for a five-a-side game. Brandt put the ball down and kicked it toward her. She ran to meet it, controlled it and passed it backward to Izzy.

Sarimah sprinted toward an open space and shouted for a return pass. Tamsen was behind her when Izzy passed the ball. It bobbled along the rough ground. Sarimah had to shield the ball. She kept possession and decided she would see how far she could go with it.

Sarimah was moving up the left wing, with Tamsen and Kaelynn in pursuit. Brandt called for a pass in the middle of the field. Sarimah pushed the ball into a space in front of him where he was alone in the middle. He banged a hard, low shot that skidded past the far post.

"Oh, great pass, Sarimah," Izzy shouted. "Come on, Brandt, you should score those ones!"

"I know!" he said.

Sarimah moved back to midfield, where she expected the ball would come after the goal kick. She was studying her teammates on the field when something caught her eye. She thought it was cotton from someone's coat or fluff floating past from a poplar tree. Then she saw another one. Suddenly, with no warning, the white flakes filled the sky.

The other team kicked the ball up the field, but Sarimah didn't notice. She was busy staring into the clouds. The snowflakes covered the ground with a thin white blanket in almost no time.

She laughed as snowflakes landed on her nose and eyelashes.

"Oh, it's finally here! Winter has arrived," Izzy said, laughing.

The other kids stopped playing to gather around Sarimah.

"You haven't seen snow before, have you?" Brandt asked.

"This is so pretty," Sarimah said. "In Syria, the tops of the mountains have snow sometimes. But I have never seen it falling from the sky."

"Yeah, it's nice now," said Izzy. "But just wait a few months and it won't look so pretty anymore. Especially when you're shovelling it ten times a day."

Sarimah turned in a circle, her face still turned up to the sky.

"Stick out your tongue and catch one," Brandt said.

Sarimah eyes lit up as snowflake after snowflake landed and melted on her eyelids and nose and tongue. She looked down and saw that everyone was watching her. Snow covered Izzy's toque and jacket. Even her eyebrows had snow on them.

"Do we have to go inside now?" Sarimah asked.

"Nah. If we let the snow stop us, we'd never get anything done," Izzy said.

"Yeah, let's go already," Tamsen said. "Recess is almost over. I'm tired of this."

"It's just some dumb snow," Kaelynn said. "What's the big deal?"

Tamsen had the ball near midfield and kicked it high toward Izzy's goal.

"Hey, no fair!" Izzy said. "We were enjoying a perfect winter moment."

"The only perfect winter moment is when winter is over," Tamsen said.

Sarimah watched as Izzy and Tamsen chased the ball. They nearly disappeared behind the snow, which was falling now in a thick sheet.

Sarimah followed down the field. She moved into an open area and called for the ball. Izzy hit it, but the ball barely made it to Sarimah. Tamsen was suddenly there. She appeared out of nowhere to challenge for the pass.

Sarimah and Tamsen collided and bumped shoulders. Tamsen slipped a little and lost her footing. She skidded down onto one knee.

"Ah! My knee," Tamsen shouted. "Watch where you're going!"

Sarimah froze. She wanted to say she was sorry, but couldn't find the right words fast enough.

"You just fell," Sarimah said.

"I did not 'just fall.' You fouled me. This is just recess, you know."

Izzy and Kaelynn came running over.

"Are you okay, Tammy?" Kaelynn asked.

"Sure, whatever. Blame me, not the refugee. It's never the fault of the refugees. Everyone is always taking their side," Tamsen said, looking at Sarimah. "The refugees are getting everything. Well, I'm not going to risk playing with someone who gets everything she wants. What if I get injured and miss provincials? Izzy, you should stop, too. We can't afford to get injured now."

Tamsen turned and stormed toward the school. Kaelynn followed close behind her.

"I just tried to get the ball," Sarimah said. "I think we just bumped lightly." She tapped her finger to Izzy's shoulder to show her.

"It's not your fault," Izzy said. "Tamsen can get excited sometimes. Soccer means everything to her."

Sarimah knew Izzy was trying to be nice, but she could see the truth. If excited was the same as rude, Tamsen was the most excited person Sarimah had ever met. As far as she was concerned, nobody should be trying to make excuses for Tamsen.

"You are friends, I know. But she is not being fair to me," Sarimah said.

"I know," Izzy said. "But I have to look out for her, sometimes. I've known her since kindergarten. Plus, she's my teammate."

Sarimah admired what Izzy was saying. Sarimah had friends who were important to her, too. But she wouldn't let a friend act like that.

"Football should be fun. School should be fun," Sarimah said. "There are too many other things to get mad about. Tamsen doesn't know how good she has it here."

5 SNOW BALL

Sarimah bobbled down the stairs and out the door. She skidded slightly on the icy pavement outside. Izzy was waiting at the end of the driveway for their walk to school.

Sarimah felt like she was ready to climb Mount Everest. Her puffy, dark grey coat with the red lining had a collar that hid her face. She had to keep pushing her scarf away from her eyes, but her slippery black mitts made it impossible to grip anything.

Her winter boots felt two sizes too big. Her bulky snow pants made a loud *whip-whip* sound as she walked. It had to be 15 degrees below zero, but she was sweating under all her layers. Sarimah tried reaching up to scratch her head under her toque. But that was just as hard as adjusting her scarf.

"You look warm," Izzy said with a smile. "But you're going to have trouble playing snow soccer in that outfit."

Sarimah tried to move her scarf, toque and hood

away from her ears. She tried to move the scarf away from her mouth as best she could. But it had frozen from her breath and she could only push it down a little.

"Will we play snow soccer today?" she finally said around her scarf.

"Yeah, probably. It's like a tradition or something. We play kickball when it rains and soccer when it snows."

"What happens if the ball gets cold?" she asked.

"When the ball gets cold, it loses its bounce. We just kick it a little harder. It's a great workout for your legs."

Sarimah couldn't hear much except their boots crunching the roadside snow. "In Syria, there would be no school in this weather. *If* we got weather like this."

"We call those snow days! It has to snow a lot more than this for us to get a snow day here."

When they rounded the last corner to school, Sarimah's eyes widened. In front of her, dozens of kids were slipping and sliding in the playground.

About ten kids were playing street hockey. She laughed when she heard little girls yelling, "Tag, you're frozen."

"When do they use those things on their feet?" she asked Izzy, pointing to the hockey players.

"You mean skates? We have to build the outdoor rink first," she said. "We usually do that just before Christmas, when it's colder."

"But it is cold now!"

Brandt appeared out of nowhere. He slid toward them, kicking up a wall of snow. "Hey, Sarimah, is it cold enough for you?"

"Yes. It is cold enough for me."

Izzy and Brandt began laughing. Sarimah couldn't help but smile, too, although she wasn't sure why.

The first bell sounded and they started toward the school. Sarimah glanced over at the soccer field. A thick blanket of snow covered it.

"Do you play soccer at lunch break?" Sarimah asked her friends.

"Of course," Brandt said. "We'll get some more people and have an even bigger game today."

Playing soccer in the snow was all Sarimah could think about during her morning classes. When it was finally noon, she grabbed her lunch from her locker and met Izzy in the cafeteria.

"How has your morning been?" Izzy asked.

"Good," Sarimah said. "What do you do in the winter?"

Izzy peeled open a yogurt container and grabbed a spoon.

"Lots of different things," she said, as she stirred. "Like I said this morning, we can't let snow stop us, or we'd never get anything done."

"Do you still go outside to play?"

"Of course. We can go out now and you'll see. Nothing changes."

"Can we play soccer in the snow?"

Izzy smiled. "How about right after we eat?"

They wolfed down their sandwiches and tossed out their recyclables before heading back to their locker. Sarimah put on her snow pants, hat, scarf, jacket, mitts and boots. She followed Izzy to the soccer field. Kids had already packed down the snow in some places. The packed-down area in front of the goal nearest to the school was almost pure ice. But Sarimah could see that other parts of the field were untouched.

Sarimah was stunned to see the same group of kids from the day before playing soccer in the snow. She shook her head. She didn't know how anyone could play soccer on snow and ice. She glanced down at her boots and tried to imagine running in them. How could she kick a ball with them?

Brandt came out of the school from a different door. He was carrying a ball. He tried to roll it to Sarimah, but it wobbled and bounced on the uneven surface. She stopped it, and realized she wasn't going to be able to do anything with it, wearing all her winter clothes.

She tried to flick the ball with her toe, but her boots were so big she just scuffed it forward.

Izzy ran up and took a shot on goal. She hit it hard, and banged it right to Seamus, who was the goal-keeper. Seamus grabbed the ball with both hands. He punted it high in the air toward the left wing.

Sarimah watched as the ball sailed high. Then it started to fall. It was as if the ball was made of stone and someone had dropped it from outer space. Sarimah expected it to bounce high and roll down the field, but instead it hit a patch of deep, soft snow.

Poof.

Only the top half of the ball was showing. It looked like the yolk of a fried egg. Kids scrambled for it, but the snow was thick and they could only lurch a step at a time. Brandt got to it first, and kicked it loose from its icy trap. He sent it back up to Izzy, who passed it back to Sarimah. Brandt rejoined them, huffing and puffing.

"Izzy, me and Sarimah will play on this side, with Seamus in goal," Brandt said. "Everyone else is on the other team."

"Wait, we're playing, too."

Sarimah looked behind her to see Tamsen and Kaelynn running up.

"Is your knee better?" Izzy asked Tamsen.

"Yeah, it's fine. Plus, I didn't like how the last game ended."

"All right, we have a game now," Brandt said. "Tamsen and Kaelynn can go on that team, but we get Derek."

Sarimah stood in the back of the group, but she heard what they were saying. She knew Tamsen was back to prove something to her.

Tamsen was wearing a short winter coat with boots that seemed half the size of Sarimah's. Sarimah watched how easily she was able to walk through the snow.

She can run in those boots much easier than I can in mine, Sarimah thought.

The kids scattered and Sarimah found herself with the ball at centre field. She wasn't sure how it was going to work. It was a big field, with just seven players per side. There would be a lot of running in the deep snow.

Sarimah tapped the ball to Brandt and the game began. He passed it back to Izzy in midfield and then went for a run. Sarimah tried to support Izzy and find some open space for a return pass.

Tamsen charged at Izzy, looking to block a pass or create a turnover.

Sarimah saw what was happening and called for the ball. She pumped her legs hard, but her boots slipped on the ice and snow. She felt like she had forgotten how to run. It was like a bad dream in which she was running as fast as she could but not going anywhere.

"Izzy, over here," she tried to yell. But her scarf muffled her words.

Izzy poked the ball back toward Brandt and they moved up the field. Sarimah turned to run into the space. But by the time she found any grip, the defence had won the ball. Sarimah was sweating under her scarf.

It went on like that for another five minutes. The ball would go over her, around her and through her. It went over her a lot. Sarimah felt like they were playing tennis, and she was the net. She was the shortest player on the field and she couldn't jump very high wearing boots.

Sarimah had barely touched the ball when the bell sounded. She thought the other kids looked like pro snow soccer players compared to her. She was exhausted and — worst of all — Tamsen's team had won 3-2.

"Looks like Canada won that one," Tamsen said.

Kaelynn snickered, but Sarimah wasn't laughing.

"Yes, it is hard to play in these," Sarimah said, lifting up her right boot. "I'm used to playing with no shoes at all." But she thought, *I will be better in summer. They will see.*

6 UP EARLY

Sarimah spent the whole night thinking about how hard it had been to play soccer in the snow. Even with all her schoolwork, the cold weather and making new friends, soccer was all she could think about. Before her alarm even went off, she awoke from a soccer dream.

She had already changed for school and was eating her breakfast by the time her father appeared in the kitchen. He poured water into the kettle and found the tea in a cupboard.

"Why are you awake this early?" he asked her, in Arabic.

"Papa, we should be practising our English," she said, in English.

He grinned and paused. She could tell he was searching for the right words.

"Okay," he answered her. "You are too good. I need time."

"Five more years, maybe," she said with a big smile.

He laughed.

"Yes, maybe," he said. "But why are you here so early?"

"I'm just excited."

He pulled a mug from the cabinet and sat down at the table. "Well, I am very glad you are starting to enjoy it here, despite the weather." This time he spoke in Arabic. He rubbed his eyes and yawned. He looked out the kitchen window. It was dark, and he shivered.

"It is okay, if you dress for it," Sarimah said. "We even play soccer in the snow."

He looked up at her and smiled. "The snow? Soccer?" he said, back in English.

Sarimah poured more cereal into her bowl and topped it with milk. She dug her spoon into the bowl and brought it to her mouth.

"It is fun," she said before chewing. "It was hard the first time, and a girl at school says I am not very good. But, now that I think about it, it's kind of like playing on the sand."

Her father laughed. "Snow is nothing like sand. There is no sunshine, no heat. Just cold."

Sarimah's dropped her shoulders a little. "That's not what I meant. I mean, the ball does the same things. Sometimes it skips, and sometimes it plunks in the snow and doesn't move. And you have to run really hard to get anywhere in the snow, just like in the sand."

He stood and moved to her. He kissed her on the forehead. "You are right. I am teasing. And it takes more energy to run around in those boots," he said, again switching back to Arabic. "Playing in the snow will make you even better after it melts — if it ever melts."

She had never thought about that. Maybe that's why she felt so good, lately. After a week of walking around in snow boots, of kicking the soccer ball in the snow, perhaps she was getting stronger. Then she started to remember all that she'd learned playing in the sand: how to run on her toes and how to use the soft ground to cushion long, loopy passes. Most important, she remembered the ball had to find the right spot. If the ball was in a hole, she had to nudge it out before trying to kick it.

Suddenly, she really wanted to get to the soccer field. She pushed away from the table and rushed to pack her bag. As she turned to get her scarf, she glanced at the clock. It was only 7:30 — too early to be leaving. She was getting dressed for the cold when her father appeared beside her. He put on this coat, hat and mitts.

"Papa, what are you doing?"

"I'm going to school, too," he said. "For my English lesson. I will walk you to school and wait until my lesson starts."

When they arrived at the schoolyard, it was still a bit dark.

"You will play in this? It is like the North Pole," her father said as he looked around.

Sarimah reached into her backpack and pulled

out the old black and white soccer ball Brandt had given her. She plunked it on the frozen field near the goalposts. In the frigid cold, it didn't bounce much. But Sarimah didn't care. Playing soccer any time felt amazing, even on a snowy, icy field in the early morning.

Sarimah turned and flicked the ball with the toe of her boot. She watched as it skidded from one hole in the snow to another. It sat low, making it hard to kick. Instead, she scuffed it forward and started to run with it. She tried to run as fast as she could while looking straight ahead. The ball bounced and wobbled, forcing her to change direction often.

When she got close enough to the goal, she tried a shot. The ball didn't go very far, and it moved slowly. She ran after it and turned to run the other way, to the opposite goal. She was nearly tired out by the time she reached midfield.

Instead of just kicking the ball from anywhere, she waited for the ball to settle on a flat space in the snow. She had to put all her strength behind the shot for it to get anywhere.

The more Sarimah tried, the better she got. Soon, she was puffing out huge clouds of frozen breath above her. She was sweating a little, and her cheeks were red and numb. She kept thinking how much easier it would be in the summer sun.

Sarimah noticed that her father was still there,

watching her. She dropped the ball and kicked it to him. He tried to knock it back, but it squibbed on a chunk of ice. They laughed together. By the time the sun was finally up, a few more kids had trickled into the schoolyard. Sarimah and her father had been practising for nearly fifteen minutes.

7 MORNING LESSONS

"What, you have a coach now?" Sarimah heard a voice say. "Well, you need it."

Sarimah didn't have to turn around to know who it was. Tamsen didn't wait for a response, either. She kept walking. Tamsen's anger hurt Sarimah even more than her words. Sarimah had cried many times since she had left Syria, but she wasn't going to do it this time.

"Who is that?" her father asked.

"Nobody," Sarimah said.

She clenched her teeth. She tensed her back and shoulders. She spotted the soccer ball and took two big strides toward it. Her right boot connected flush and sent the ball rocketing forward. It hit the crossbar and bounced straight down before rolling across the goal line.

Maybe I should play angry more often, she thought.

"Great shot, Sarimah. You should play angry more often," her father said.

"How do you know I am angry?"

"I heard you growling. *Grrr*! I figured you were angry, or hungry. And I saw you eat breakfast, so I know you are not hungry."

Sarimah felt better, even though a couple of tears had rolled down her cheek.

"If you cry, your tears will freeze. How can you see the ball with frozen eyes?" her father said gently.

Sarimah shuffled from one foot to the next, not making eye contact with her father.

"What did that girl say to upset you? She talks too fast."

"She thinks I need help to play soccer well."

"Everyone needs help to get better."

"I just want to play. I want to be better at snow soccer."

Her father let out a sigh. Sarimah watched as his breath froze in the air above his head.

"I think that girl is not happy," he said. "But that does not mean you should let her make you not happy."

Sarimah's expression softened. She looked at her father and smiled.

"Thank you. You are right."

He picked up Sarimah's backpack for her. They walked toward the school, arm in arm.

"I have to go," he said. "It is freezing. Do not worry about soccer, on snow or not. Soccer is just fun."

She kissed him goodbye. Their morning together

reminded her how thankful she was for having a father like hers. Who else would leave home early just to kick a ball in the snow? She promised herself she would remember what he said. Soccer is supposed to be fun, not make you cry.

Soon after, Brandt and Izzy showed up for school. All three kicked the ball back and forth a little before the bell rang. They promised to play on the same team at lunchtime.

When they came outside after morning classes, the wind howled and they all braced themselves. Brandt shivered and pulled up the zipper on his jacket. Sarimah thought she had never been colder in her life.

"We need to run," she said.

"It's pretty cold out today," Brandt said. "I don't think anyone is going to join us."

Sarimah chased after the ball. She pushed it to where it could rest on a flat space.

"How about penalty shots? We all take turns?"

Brandt backed into the goal area between the posts.

"Okay, but let's hurry," he said.

Sarimah marched off the twelve yards and dug her heel into the snow.

"This is the place."

She fiddled with the ball a little. It kept slipping on the ice. Finally, it came to a rest just behind the penalty spot. She backed up her usual two paces and began her run.

When she got to the ball, Sarimah swung her leg. She tried to make good contact without slipping. Her boot connected flush, but there wasn't much power behind her shot. The ball curled to Brandt's left. He was able to shuffle just a few steps and block it with his right foot.

"Next!"

He tossed the ball back to the girls at the penalty spot. Izzy placed it to the left of the mark. She backed up five or six yards and started a slow run. She booted it high into the air. It looped to Brandt's left side this time. He moved under it and caught it as it came down.

"Yes, I'm perfect in goal!" he shouted.

He switched places with Izzy and placed the ball in front of the penalty mark.

"Hey, that is cheating! Mine was from way back here," Sarimah said with a grin.

She walked toward Brandt and showed him where she had placed the ball.

"That's all icy," he said. "No one can score from there."

He moved left to where the snow was stickier. As he approached the ball, he planted his left foot in some crunchy, hard snow. He slammed the ball hard. It looped perfectly and scored inside the right post.

"Wow! I am so amazing! I totally knew it was going to do that," he said.

"Sure you did! Remember, you were so much

closer to goal," Izzy shouted. She kicked the ball to Sarimah and took her place in goal.

Sarimah tried to do just what Brandt had done. She approached the ball in the same way and scored the same way.

"Hey, this isn't fair! You are ganging up on me," Izzy said.

Sarimah and Brandt started laughing.

"Okay, Sarimah, your turn to go in goal." Izzy traded places with Sarimah.

"I am not tall," Sarimah said with a smile. "So do not kick it so high."

"Don't try to trick me," Brandt said. "I know what you're trying to do. You want me to take it easy on you. But if I score here, I win."

Sarimah jumped up and down, trying to distract Brandt. He put the ball in the same place he had scored from before. He moved to the side and started his run. Sarimah kept jumping. She jumped to her right. She dove, knowing the soft snow would protect her fall.

The ball curled just beyond Sarimah's reach.

"Goooaaalll!" Brandt yelled. "Sarimah, you are a great player, but not such a good goalie."

Sarimah picked herself up off the ground. She watched as Brandt did an elaborate goal celebration dance. He waved his arms from side to side like a hula dancer from Hawaii as he tiptoed through the snow.

"I am *what*?" she asked him.

He stopped.

"You're not such a great goalie," he said. "Not against me, anyway. Then again, who is? Ha-ha-ha!"

"No, the other thing."

"Oh, you are a great player," Brandt said. He and Izzy walked toward her.

"I am?"

"Yes, you are a great soccer player. Didn't you know that?"

"No, I did not." Sarimah brushed the snow from her knees.

"Well, somebody should have told you a long time ago," Brandt said.

8 SOMETHING TO CHEW ON

Every time Sarimah left the classroom, she felt like she was walking through a forest. She couldn't see over anyone's head. She was pretty sure that she was shorter than anyone else her age.

"Hey, Sarimah, let's go play soccer," Izzy shouted, in the crowded hallway.

Sarimah heard her voice, but had to stand on her tippy-toes to find her. Little kids spun around her. Older kids towered over her. She had to nudge her way through the crowd to their locker. She felt like was walking through tall grass that was in her way.

"You need to use your elbows a little more," Izzy said, laughing. "I'm sure you don't get pushed around like that on the soccer field."

They walked to the lunchroom together, where they found Brandt and Seamus. They sat down at the table with the boys.

"How many bites do you think I can eat my sandwich in?" Brandt asked.

"Four," Seamus said.

"No problem," Brandt answered.

"Okay, but no milk or water or anything."

"If I do it, I get your cookies."

"Deal, but if I win, I get your cupcake."

Sarimah watched as Brandt took two huge bites. He chewed slowly, with his cheeks puffed out like a squirrel. He swallowed hard.

"That's two," Brandt said. "Only two more allowed."

He took another big bite, and suddenly stopped.

"Nobody give him anything to drink!" Seamus shouted excitedly. He stood up to watch Brandt closely. "I'm going to get his dessert, I know it."

Sarimah started to laugh. The look on Brandt's face was a mixture of panic and joy.

"Make him laugh, make him laugh!" Seamus shouted.

Brandt braced his hands against the table. He was laughing now and trying to keep the sandwich in his mouth. Finally, he grabbed his milk and took a huge swig.

"Yes! I win," Seamus said. "Hand over your cookies, buddy."

"I shouldn't have brought tuna salad on brown bread today," Brandt said.

"What were you thinking? You didn't stand a chance."

"Wait," Sarimah said. "I can do three bites. Then I get the cookies."

Sarimah wasn't sure what she had gotten herself into. But it looked like fun.

"Okay," Izzy said. "What do we get if you can't?"

Sarimah thought for a second.

"I will bring you baklava," she said. "It is from Syria. It has lots of honey and pastry."

"I don't know how to say that. But it sounds delicious," Brandt said. "You have a deal."

Sarimah picked up her sandwich. She took a huge bite.

"Whoa, awesome," Izzy shouted.

Sarimah finished off the rest of the sandwich in two more bites. Izzy, Brandt and Seamus all clapped.

"I was hungry. It helps with tomato and lettuce," Sarimah said, taking the cookies. "Not so sticky."

"Okay, let's go outside or something," Izzy said. She stood up to leave.

Sarimah jumped to her feet. She scooped up all her containers and tossed them into her lunch bag. Before she could get out of the lunchroom, she had to get around another group of kids. How had her friends already made it to the lunchroom door?

"You going to practise soccer? Don't you need to call in your personal coach?"

Sarimah remained silent for a few seconds. She was alone in front of Tamsen again. She watched as her friends walked ahead of her into the hallway.

"We are all going to play," she said. "Will you come?"

"I doubt it. It's not real soccer. Not like with my indoor soccer team, the Blizzard. I don't want to waste my time playing with just anyone in the snow."

Sarimah's stomach flipped. She tried her best to smile. They stood in silence for a few seconds. Then Izzy rushed back into the lunchroom.

"Hey, Sarimah, let's go. What's taking you so long? Lunch is going to be over soon," Izzy said.

Sarimah let out a big breath.

"Tammy, we need another player," Izzy said. "Come on."

"Maybe," Tamsen said. Sarimah saw that she didn't want to let Izzy down. They were teammates on the Blizzard. "Okay, I'll show you all how to really play."

They met up outside. Tamsen was wearing her sleek winter boots and slim jacket. Sarimah was in her second-hand parka and oversized boots. She felt clumsy. But she didn't want to let it stop her. She bent over and tied up her bootlaces as tight as possible. It made her feel much better about running in the snow. She took off her jacket.

"Why don't you just unzip the liner and wear that?" Brandt said.

Sarimah looked at him, and then at her jacket.

He picked it up for her. "My brother has this same jacket," he said.

He found the inside zipper, undid it and pulled the jacket apart. He handed a smaller, red jacket to Sarimah.

"There. Now, what are the teams?" he asked.

Sarimah was amazed. She had not realized there was another piece to her coat. She waved her arms around. She had more freedom to move!

"You four over there against us four over here," Seamus said. He motioned to Sarimah, Tamsen, Izzy and Brandt as a team. "We'll play half-field."

Sarimah had not expected to be on Tamsen's team. She wondered how Tamsen felt about it.

Seamus grabbed the ball and booted it high from the goal area. It hadn't snowed for a couple of days, so the snow on the field was packed down. It made it icier than before. The ball skipped and slid from one end of the field to the other. It didn't matter what kind of boots anyone was wearing. Sarimah could see everyone was having trouble standing. It made it tough to score, and the teams managed just two goals each as the game continued.

"Whoa, look out below!" Brandt shouted. He took a running start at a huge slide for the ball.

He nudged it forward to where Sarimah could get it. She scooted off to the wing with the ball. There was some empty space there. Then Tamsen broke through the middle of the field. Sarimah acted quickly and punched a pass up to her. Tamsen ran onto the ball and nudged it into the goal. It was a *whizz-bang* play that caught everyone by surprise.

"Amazing play, you two," Izzy said.

"Nice pass," Tamsen said. But she glanced past Sarimah, instead of looking at her.

"It was a good run," Sarimah added.

It was the best play of the game, and the last. The bell rang and the game was over.

"Hey, we win 3-2," Brandt said. "Tammy gets the winner, with an assist to Sarimah!"

The two teams gathered and all the players walked back into the school.

"Sarimah and Tamsen, what a great combo," Izzy added. "You two have good chemistry."

Sarimah looked over at Tamsen, who didn't seem to have heard what Izzy had said. Tamsen walked away without saying anything.

"I'm serious," Izzy said to Sarimah. "You guys are both so smart. I bet if you joined our team, you two would be amazing together."

Sarimah looked at Izzy. She wasn't sure if she was joking or not.

"Well, yes, I would like that," Sarimah said finally. "It would be amazing."

9 GYM CLASS

Everyone in Sarimah's Grade 7 gym class gathered at the doors. The teacher appeared from around a corner. He asked them to form a single line and head outside quietly.

"You voted to play snow soccer for gym class," he said. "Everyone who has a light-coloured jacket will play on one team. Everyone with a dark-coloured jacket is on the other."

Sarimah looked down at her red coat liner and then at Izzy's silver jacket. She glanced around at the other kids and noticed Brandt and Seamus both wearing light colours, too. She spotted Kaelynn and Tamsen standing together, in black jackets.

"Sarimah," the gym teacher said, "you'll play with the dark jackets to even the teams."

"I guess we will be playing against each other," Izzy said.

"I guess, yes."

Sarimah was amazed at how warm the sun felt.

It was almost like spring. She shielded her eyes and looked around.

"It's nice out, isn't it?" Izzy said. "It doesn't happen that often. But we're happy when it does. It's a Chinook."

"What is that?"

"It's when a whole bunch of warm air comes from the mountains. That's why we're outside for gym class."

"Yesterday was so cold," Sarimah said. "I do not understand."

"Welcome to Canada. You don't like the weather, wait ten minutes," Izzy answered. "At least that's what my grandpa says."

The class made two teams of ten players each. It was the most players Sarimah had seen on the school field. Tamsen called her team together and started putting people into positions. She said she would play forward, while Kaelynn would play centre midfield. She sent Sarimah to play right midfield.

The teacher placed a ball at centre and flipped a coin. Tamsen called *tails*.

"Heads, so the 'Silver Stars' win," he called. "The 'Dark Knights' have to defend."

Sarimah watched the other team kick the ball back to their midfield. Brandt suddenly scooped up some snow and made a snowball. He tossed it at Tamsen and then ran for cover behind the teacher.

"Snowballs are fair play!" Brandt shouted.

"Quit it!" Tamsen yelled. "Take the game seriously."

Kaelynn moved into position behind Tamsen. Sarimah moved beside and to the right of the two girls. She could see they wanted to pressure the ball. She would help by cutting off any passes to her side of the field.

She moved closer to the middle, knowing it would be hard for the other team to kick the ball over her head. It was warmer, but still below freezing. The ball wouldn't sail as high as it would in warm weather.

The plan worked well. Tamsen forced the Silver Stars to kick the ball all the way back to Izzy in centre defence. Izzy had to retreat to her left, with Tamsen in pursuit. Kaelynn cut off the middle, so Izzy tried to kick the ball up the field.

She wound up and swung as hard as she could. The ball went up into the air. Then it came down almost as quickly. Sarimah was in the perfect place to trap it. Tamsen made a diagonal run in front of Izzy.

Sarimah took a quick dribble so the ball wasn't sitting too low. She popped it forward, right into Tamsen's path. Tamsen had nobody in front of her except the goalie. She scored, making it look easy, with a side-footed shot into the net.

"Wow," Brandt said. "That was the fastest goal in Thornton Park School history!"

The teams regrouped for another kick-off at centre.

This time, the Silver Stars tried kicking the ball forward, away from Tamsen and Sarimah.

Izzy moved ahead from centre defence, leaving a huge space behind her. Sarimah thought if she could just get the ball, she would be able to kick it ahead to Tamsen again. It would be another sure goal. Sarimah watched in amazement as Izzy kept running to the far side of the field where the ball was.

"She is not playing smart," Sarimah said. But nobody was close enough to hear her.

But somehow, it worked. Izzy stole the ball and charged toward the goal. A few kids were giving chase, but mostly people just let her run past them. Izzy would kick the ball into empty space. It would splat in some soft snow and she would chase up to it, and kick it again. She continued like that most of the way down the whole field.

"This is silly," Sarimah said.

"Hey, don't be so slow!" Tamsen yelled from the forward position.

"Yes, I agree," Sarimah said.

Her other teammates didn't seem nearly as concerned. Izzy deked past one and then another until she was right in the penalty area. At least, it was what Sarimah thought was the penalty area. With all the snow, she couldn't see any lines. Sarimah finally decided she had better move back to help defend, when Izzy unleashed a wicked shot. It curled left and then down before it scored.

"Toe-bomb!" she said, cheering.

"It's good to have big snow boots," Brandt said, as they high-fived.

Kaelynn and Tamsen kicked off at centre. They booted it back to Sarimah on the right wing. The three formed a triangle and moved the ball up-field. Brandt and Izzy played defence just enough to slow them down.

Then, Sarimah made a run up the right side. She was at the side of the field farthest from the school. The snow there hadn't been touched. Kaelynn spotted her and hammered the ball ahead as hard as she could. Sarimah ran onto it, with Brandt close behind. He wasn't slowing down and Sarimah was worried he was going to try something funny. She almost expected him to throw a snowball at her.

But Sarimah caught up to the ball and dug her toe underneath it, just as she had in the sand. Brandt let out a yell and came sliding forward. Sarimah flicked the ball high into the air and it looped over Brandt. Sarimah watched Brandt slide on the wet, slippery snow — much farther than Hassan had at the refugee camp. The ball bounced and Sarimah continued her chase. Izzy managed to get back into position. But in front of Sarimah it was just Izzy, and then Seamus in goal.

Sarimah continued to run toward the goal, forcing Izzy to come in to defend her closely. That helped

Sarimah decide. She passed the ball on a sharp angle in front of the net. Kaelynn ran onto it and kicked home the go-ahead goal.

"Amazing goal, Kaelynn," Tamsen said, running to congratulate her friend.

"But what about that pass?" someone yelled.

Kaelynn and Tamsen stopped and looked around. A man was standing off to the side of the goal. Kaelynn put her hand above her eyes to shield them from the sun.

"Coach?"

Sarimah stayed back a little. Izzy, Kaelynn and Tamsen ran to greet him. Sarimah was suddenly nervous, but she wasn't sure why.

10 OPEN INVITATION

Izzy, Tamsen, and Kaelynn walked behind the goal to greet the visitor. Sarimah watched them closely. She didn't think he was a teacher.

"Sorry," Izzy said to the gym teacher. "Can we have a break to talk to our coach?" At a nod from the teacher, she turned to Sarimah. "Hey, Sarimah, come here for a second."

"Are you sure, Sarimah?" Brandt said. "Your team will be missing your three best players."

"Well, then you better score," Kaelynn said. Everyone was watching Sarimah as she approached the group behind the goal. The man was smiling, but Tamsen was not.

"Coach, this is Sarimah," Izzy said, smiling. "She's the one who made that brilliant pass. She's the one I told you about the other day."

"*As-Salaam-Alaikum,*" the man said.

Sarimah gasped. How could someone be giving her the traditional Muslim greeting? She never thought she would hear Arabic in the schoolyard at Thornton Park.

"*Wa-Alaikum-Salaam*," she said, stuttering a little.

"My name is Krisna, but everyone just calls me *Kris* or *Coach K*," the man said. "I'm sorry my Arabic is not good. I am from Indonesia, but I have lived here twenty-five years."

Sarimah was still unsure of what to say. She could feel everyone staring at them.

"That was a beautiful play, very creative," Coach K said when Sarimah remained silent. "Where did you learn that?"

Sarimah looked down at her boots. She was a little embarrassed, but thinking about soccer made her braver.

"In the sand in Turkey," she said. "Playing on snow is almost the same."

The man smiled. "I suppose it is almost the same — minus the sunshine."

"That's what my father said."

"How are you enjoying Canada, Sarimah? It took me a long time to settle in here when I arrived. I still miss my home often."

Sarimah looked up at him and smiled. It made her feel good to hear that others missed their homes, too. It made her think of what her family had left behind in Aleppo.

"I miss it, yes," she said. "But Canada is nice. My friends are nice."

"That's very important. I'm glad my players are welcoming you."

"You are their coach?"

"Yes, I coach the Blizzard. I would love to have you as a guest at practice tonight, if your parents say it's okay."

Sarimah thought about playing indoors, with no snow, in the warmth. She couldn't keep in her happiness. A smile spread across her face.

Tamsen turned suddenly and looked at her coach. Kaelynn mumbled something.

"Coach, we already picked our team," Tamsen said. "We can't add anyone."

Coach K held up a hand. "She will be our guest," he said. "Tamsen is right, though. We are nearing the deadline to add any players. But this will just be a friendly offer, from neighbours to new friends to make her feel welcome."

Izzy came over to Sarimah's side and mussed her toque a little. She was still smiling from ear to ear.

"Besides, Tamsen," coach said, "it looks like you and Sarimah have a good connection. Maybe you want her passing to you more often?"

Tamsen turned away from them. The gym teacher came over to the group.

"You going to join us, Kris?" the teacher asked. "We'd love to see your moves."

Coach K laughed. "It looks like fun. But I can't

stay," he said. "I just came here to drop off a thank-you letter to the school, for supporting our team. I have to get back to work. But I'm glad I came to say hello first."

Coach K turned and walked back toward the parking lot. Sarimah wanted to scream with joy.

She couldn't help smiling all day, from the time the gym class ended until the final bell sounded.

When Sarimah got home, there was a bag of clothes sitting outside the front door. Attached was a note. It said, "To Sarimah, thought you might want these." It was signed '*Mo.*'

Their sponsors had already given them a TV, radio, clothes, shoes and books. But Sarimah's family had found clothes and household items on their doorstep before. The neighbours often dropped off gifts for them. Once, Sarimah came home from school to find an entire set of dishes, and then pots and pans the next day. They looked like nobody had ever used them. At first, Sarimah wondered how Canadians could afford to buy them such nice things.

Her teacher told her that many families had more than they need. Their neighbours were just giving them what they didn't use. That puzzled Sarimah even more.

She turned her attention to the new supplies. She opened the bag, expecting to see another scarf or a pair of mittens. Instead, she pulled out three pairs of soccer socks, shorts, and two jerseys — one white and the other green. They said 'University of Saskatchewan Huskies' on them. Then Sarimah pulled out running pants and a long-sleeved T-shirt. At the bottom was a set of shin pads and a pair of soccer cleats.

Sarimah upended the bag to get the pads and cleats out. She put the cleats on and wiggled her toes. They were a little big. *But wearing two pairs of socks would make them just about right, and leave her some room to grow,* she thought.

"Nice!" she said.

"What now?" Her mother had heard her come in.

"Look, Mama. Mohammed left this for me," Sarimah said, in Arabic.

"What is all this? For football?"

"Yes. Now I don't have to borrow anything from Izzy."

Her mother picked up the plastic bag and looked at the handwritten note. Then she opened the bag and peered inside.

"Mama, it's an empty bag. There's nothing hiding in there," Sarimah said, laughing.

Her mother wrinkled her brow at Sarimah. "Don't tease me," she said. "Where are you going to use those shoes? You can't wear them in the snow."

"For indoor soccer. Izzy's team asked me to practise with them tonight. I will go with Izzy and her mother in their car."

Her mother's eyes darkened. Sarimah realized she

should have asked permission first. She held her breath.

"On a school night?" her mother said. "You should be studying. This is not a good idea."

"Please, Mama," Sarimah said.

Her mother sighed. "Your father will be home soon. Let him decide."

Sarimah collected all her new soccer clothes and carried them to her room. She put them out on the bed. She put the running pants and long-sleeved T-shirt on first. They were stretchy and thin. She managed to put on her soccer clothes — shorts, jersey and socks — over them. She still felt like she could move freely. Into her backpack, she tucked away the shin pads and shoes.

She returned into the living room just as her father returned home.

"Hello, Papa," she said. "I have something to ask you."

11 TEA FOR THREE

Sarimah's father hung his coat in the hallway before kicking off his boots and heading to the kitchen.

"I need tea," he said. "This weather — I tell you. And today everyone said it was warm outside. If this is warm, I am a camel."

He began filling the kettle with water and found the teapot. He placed his mug on the counter. Then he turned to see his wife and daughter staring at him.

"I feel like something happened while I was away," he said as he got the tea from the cupboard.

"Papa, can I play football with Izzy? She plays on an all-girls team. The coach is Muslim."

His father looked up as he searched for a spoon in the drawer. When he found one, he placed it next to the mug.

"What? Football? Why? Where is all this coming from?"

"I met the coach today at school. He asked me to come to practice."

She watched as her father stared at the kettle.

"Will this cost money?" he asked.

"No, he asked me just for practices. Izzy's mother will drive me."

"Who is this coach and what is this team? Where do you play, outside?"

Sarimah smiled. She knew her father was joking. At least she hoped he was.

"Papa, you are being silly. I'm going to the indoor Soccer Centre. The team is called the Blizzard."

"Good name."

Sarimah's mother moved to the kitchen table and sat down.

"She wants to go tonight," her mother said.

"Tonight? It's a school night. I don't want you playing on school nights."

Sarimah's shoulders slumped. She flopped into a chair next to her mother. She folded her arms on the table and rested her head on them. All Sarimah could hear was water heating in the kettle. Then the kettle started to whistle. No one said anything as her father poured hot water into the teapot.

Sarimah's mind was racing. She was so close to finally playing football on a real pitch. She didn't want to push her father for an answer too quickly. But she didn't want to give up, either.

Then she thought of the refugee camp.

"Papa, remember what you said to me in Turkey?"

He was slowly stirring the tea. "I told you many things."

"It was when we heard that our old neighbourhood had been attacked. You said it was the worst day of your life. You wanted to know why you couldn't provide a safe home for your family."

She could see he remembered, by the look that crossed his face. He poured two cups of tea and joined them at the table. He passed one cup to his wife.

"I will never forget that day," he said sadly.

"You said you would do anything for me, to make me safe and happy. Papa, playing football will make me happy. I want this more than anything I've ever wanted before. I will be safe. I won't let it interfere with my school work."

The only sound in the room was the ticking of their clock. Sarimah counted forty-four seconds before her father said anything.

"You are precious to me. Our only gift from God," he said. "We risked much to get here. So I don't want anything to happen to you now. You are getting older. Just because we are in Canada now doesn't mean we forget where we came from . . ."

Sarimah stood and walked over to her father. She was worried he wouldn't let her play without covering up and showing proper respect to Islam.

"Papa, look. I will be dressed respectfully."

She showed him the running pants, the long socks

and the long-sleeved shirt. He patted her shoulder.

"Yes, that is important. But you have always been respectful to our faith," he said. "I am not worried about that."

Sarimah was confused. She didn't understand why he was hesitating. He turned his attention to his tea again. She could tell he was thinking.

"This girl, the one from the school," he said after awhile. "She doesn't like you? How are the others treating you? And where did you get all this equipment? We don't need to accept all these gifts."

Now it was Sarimah's turn to think. She didn't want to worry her father. But she also had to be honest with him.

"You mean Tamsen," she said. "No, she is not kind like Izzy. Everyone else has been very nice, though."

He took a sip of his tea and placed the cup gently down on the table. "You think playing football with her will help you? It doesn't seem possible."

Sarimah started to feel better. Maybe her father was warming to the idea. *He hasn't said no yet,* she thought. "The last time we played soccer, we were on the same team. She even said I made a nice pass to her."

Her mother shifted in her seat. "Football, always football," she said. "Your schooling in the refugee camp was not good. You must catch up."

Sarimah was ready with an answer. But she paused, not wanting to sound anxious. "It's only one practice,

Mama. And soccer helps my English. You have to speak quickly on the field. I'm learning words that I wouldn't get to use in school."

Her parents looked at each other. Her mother finished her tea and poured some more. She sighed and stared at Sarimah's father.

"Okay, I know that look," her father said. "I guess it will be up to me. When are you supposed to be leaving?"

Sarimah's heart skipped a beat. In her mind, her father not saying no was just as good as "Yes, you can play." But she tried to stay calm.

"Izzy is hoping to come for me in about ten minutes. We will be back just after eight o'clock."

Without saying a word, Sarimah's parents walked down the hallway to their bedroom. Sarimah sat at the table, not moving. She figured if she didn't say anything — if she didn't make a sound — she might stand a better chance of getting permission.

All she could do was count the seconds on the clock and wait. She lost track at 222.

What can they be talking about? she wondered. *Why don't they just tell me, already?*

12 SELECT FEW

Sarimah sprinted out the door. She didn't turn around. She kept moving forward, in case her father changed his mind. She jumped happily into the car.

"I guess this means you are allowed to come?" Izzy asked her. "Or, you're running away from home, and this is the getaway car?"

Sarimah laughed loudly. She couldn't remember laughing like that since before she had left Syria.

"Yes, I can play," she said. "My parents say we will talk about it some more. But right now, this is good enough for me."

When they finally approached the indoor sports centre, Sarimah couldn't wait to get inside. She jumped from the car and led the way into the building. She grabbed the door handle and stepped inside. She was stunned by all the activity.

Izzy led her through the lobby and down hallways. "There are four soccer fields, a bunch of volleyball courts and lots of dressing rooms," Izzy said. "We're down at the end. There are lots of places to watch right on the field, or you can watch from up here."

Most walls had notices or sign-up sheets for soccer, volleyball or football. Sarimah stared from the viewing area as kids of all ages criss-crossed on the turf below. All of them wore flashy orange, blue or yellow shoes. They all had matching jerseys and kicked shiny new soccer balls at nets that were bright with orange mesh.

Izzy and Sarimah weaved through moms, dads, coaches and players to find Izzy's teammates. They were gathered at the field level, putting on their cleats. The group looked over at Izzy, and then to Sarimah.

"Hey, everyone, this is Sarimah," Izzy said. "She goes to our school and Coach K invited her to practise with us. She moved here from Syria."

Sarimah raised her hand and then brought it down again. The girls were all wearing yellow shirts that said 'Blizzard Under-13 Girls.' They waved back at Sarimah. Some of them came forward to welcome her. Sarimah tried to remember all the girls' names. She scanned their faces until she found Tamsen, who was standing near the coach.

"Come on, team. We've only got forty-five minutes. Let's get moving," Coach K said.

Sarimah sat down and brushed her hand over the artificial turf. She was amazed at how bouncy it felt. She put her shoes on and joined the team for fifteen minutes of warm-up exercises. She was sweating, but happy to be moving without heavy winter boots. She was able to bounce on her toes and pass the ball with ease on the flat surface.

The coach grabbed red pinnies from the team's equipment bag and tossed them to half the team. Sarimah and Izzy got pinnies, which they put on over their shirts. Tamsen was with the girls who wore just their yellow Blizzard shirts.

Finally, Sarimah thought, *a game.*

"It's seven on seven. Red jerseys at this end with me," Coach K instructed. "I'll play goal here. Marty will play goal for the yellow team."

The coach grabbed a game ball from the sideline and dribbled back to his goal crease. "Okay, let's go!"

Sarimah sprinted hard toward him, looking for an easy pass. But the coach booted it the length of the field to Marty in the other goal. Sarimah could only watch as the ball sailed high over her head.

"Your team starts," Coach K said to Marty.

Okay, so we're on defence, Sarimah thought. She turned and made her way slowly up-field.

The six attacking players on each team divided into three up front and three in the back. Sarimah found herself along the sideline in defence, at left full-back.

Team Yellow knocked the ball back to the goal-tender. She reversed it to the opposite side, away from Sarimah. She tracked a Yellow forward toward her goal as Tamsen smacked a crossing pass toward Coach

K in goal. Sarimah jumped as high as she could, but she wasn't able to reach the ball. The forward was much taller than Sarimah. She managed to head the ball on goal. It spun wildly off her head, forcing the coach to dive to his right to make a save.

"Nice header!" he said after corralling the ball.

Sarimah was angry with herself. She had been in the right position. But she was the shortest girl on the field. She stood no chance against a taller opponent.

As everyone clapped, Sarimah spun and found some open space back on her left wing. She wanted to prove herself. The coach saw her break and he faked a clearing pass. He rolled the ball to Sarimah, who controlled it and took two big strides. She looked up to see Giorgianna streaking up the middle. Sarimah slammed a hard pass through the centre of the field.

Giorgianna split the defence and was wide open, but the ball scooted past her. Sarimah's pass was too hard. She hadn't expected it to roll so fast. The ball went right to the yellow team's goalie.

"Gotta watch that fast turf," the coach shouted.

"That's two mistakes!" Sarimah scolded herself.

Team Yellow pushed some passes around before charging forward up the right wing. This time, Sarimah was ready. She bumped shoulders with Lisa, hoping to keep her from leaping for the ball.

Tamsen's cross came, but this time there was nobody to connect with it. The ball scooted out of bounds.

"Hey, Sarimah bumped me. That's a foul!" Lisa shouted.

Sarimah looked at Coach K.

"You can bump shoulders. Play on," he said. "You have to be tough, Lisa! Fight through those defenders."

Sarimah ran to the sidelines to retrieve the ball for a throw-in. She picked it up and tossed it ahead to Molly, who hit it back to Sarimah.

Sarimah took a step back with the ball and passed it to Coach K in goal. Tamsen was right there, so the coach had to slam the ball up-field in a hurry.

"*Argh!*" Sarimah shouted. She had almost turned over the ball right in front of her goal. She hadn't seen Tamsen sneaking around.

That's three mistakes, she thought. *They'll never have me back.*

She looked up-field. The yellow team was trying the same play. Sarimah stuck to their team's forward, and Tamsen didn't try a cross. Instead, Tamsen passed the ball back to the defence. They were coming to Sarimah's wing.

Sarimah shuffled across, following the ball. She waited for the pass along the sidelines.

Suddenly, Sarimah saw a flash of yellow. Tamsen was making a run through the middle, behind her. Sarimah looked up again to see the other team's defender preparing her pass. Sarimah darted into the middle of the field and intercepted the ball.

It was right on her foot, right in stride.

She charged forward, glancing up to see Marty at the top of her goal crease. Sarimah didn't think twice. She dug down deep and smashed a shot that curled high into the air. It looped over the goalie's head. Marty ran backward, trying to get into position.

The ball dipped under the crossbar and scored. Sarimah jumped in the air and pumped her fist. She heard the people in the balcony give a surprised shout. Everyone watching — the parents and the other coaches — clapped. She looked up at the balcony, and then down at her feet. She was just across the halfway line.

"I like this turf," she said.

13 PAPA'S OLD SHOES

The doorbell rang and Sarimah grabbed her soccer gear.

"There must be a fire in there," Izzy said as Sarimah rushed out the door.

"We must hurry. Practice must start on time. If we are late coming home, then Papa becomes . . ." Sarimah paused ". . . like the monster in the trash can."

"Oscar the Grouch?"

"Exactly. Papa becomes the grouch."

They raced to the car. Izzy scurried to the other side while Sarimah grabbed the closest door handle and flopped into the back seat.

"Step on it, mom."

Izzy's mother turned. "What's the rush?" she asked.

"We must be home before six. My father is at English class," Sarimah said.

"Is that bad?"

"Well, he does not like English class. If I am home when he gets home, I can help him. Then maybe he will let me keep playing football. He calls English the language of . . . well, I should not say. It is not nice."

"Tell us!" Izzy said.

"He calls it the 'language of farm animals.' He says it would be easier to learn how to speak with cows and sheep."

Izzy's mother burst out laughing. She was still chuckling when they arrived at the Soccer Centre. Sarimah didn't think it was that funny. But she knew she still had things to learn about English, too. Especially what people thought was funny.

Once they arrived, the girls sprinted into the Soccer Centre. They rushed through the change-room door and collapsed into a corner of the room, laughing the entire way.

Izzy threw her track pants into a heap. She pulled her socks up so fast she heard them rip. Sarimah stepped into her cleats and yanked at her laces. They headed out as fast as they had arrived, leaning on each other. They barely fit through the door, and spilled onto the turf like a couple of puppies.

Sarimah's shin pads were almost falling out of her socks. Izzy's shirt was inside out.

"I don't want to know," Coach K said, looking at them. "You two should take some laps to get warmed up."

"We have been running already," Sarimah said. This triggered another bout of giggling.

The leftover laughing didn't help them kick the

ball. Sarimah's shots sailed high. Izzy's passes dribbled wide. Sarimah stopped laughing once she stubbed her toe. She bent down to rub her left foot.

"Maybe if you weren't wearing your father's old cleats, you'd kick the ball better," Tamsen said, trotting past.

The more Sarimah thought about the insult, the angrier she got. She stared at the other girls on the team. They all had bright yellow or electric-blue shoes. They were so bright she thought they must glow in the dark. The other girls had shiny soccer shorts and extra-thick shin pads.

Sarimah looked down at her own legs. She looked at the heavy black cleats. She saw shin pads that looked like they wouldn't protect her from a light breeze.

Who cares? she thought. *In Syria, I would play barefoot if I had to. In Turkey, we had to play barefoot. No one brought shoes when they escaped from Syria.*

Sarimah could feel her chest tighten. She clenched both her hands into fists.

Finally, it was her turn in a three-on-two drill. She exploded from the line.

"Here I am!"

Her shout startled Giorgianna so much she passed to Sarimah without thinking. Sarimah took two strides and blasted the ball as hard as she could.

The ball dipped and swerved, and hit the back of the goal.

"Yeah!" She remembered how well she played when she was angry.

She jogged back into line. As she passed Tamsen, she slowed down a little. "I guess there are still some goals left in Papa's old shoes," she said.

Coach K blew his whistle and divided the team into two. Sarimah and Izzy were together, with Tamsen and Kaelynn.

"You'll be the Thornton School connection," the coach said as he tossed them the red pinnies.

The teams separated and the play started. The yellow team kicked the ball all the way back to Marty in goal. Sarimah wanted the ball. When the yellow team put the ball into the centre of the field, Sarimah took a chance. She sprinted up to double-team Rosy and then stepped in front of a pass for an easy steal.

"Sarimah!" Tamsen shouted.

Tamsen was on a full sprint up the field. Sarimah could see a wide-open lane and she hit the ball. Tamsen collected it and charged into the goal area. The defender slowed Tamsen enough that Sarimah had time to catch them.

"Tammy!" she yelled from the right wing.

Tamsen passed to Sarimah, who faked a shot. She passed across the goal to Kaelynn on the left wing. Kaelynn scored into an empty goal.

"Why didn't you shoot, Sarimah?" Marty cried, throwing her hands in the air. "I was ready for a shot!"

"Nice play, everyone!" Tamsen said.

Sarimah smiled at Tamsen and Kaelynn as they headed back to their side of the field. Their team went on to win the game 4-0.

Sarimah noticed a difference in her teammates after the intense practice. In the change room, they asked Sarimah what she liked best about Canada. She asked them about soccer in the summertime. Sarimah felt like she belonged.

"I love your hair colour," she told Molly. "It is like the sun setting."

"Oh, okay, that's awesome. You're my new best friend now."

They were chatting happily when Coach K shouted into the room.

"I need Tamsen, Marty and Izzy out here, please."

"Team captains," Izzy said. "Let's go."

"What are they going to talk about?" Sarimah asked Molly.

"Probably something about the city finals," she said. "They're coming up soon."

Sarimah finished changing and walked outside the change room. Some of the parents had arrived on the field level.

"Great playing out there," one woman said. "I'm Lisa's mom."

"Thank you," Sarimah said.

"We are all happy you're here and safe. It's tragic

what's happening to your country."

"Yes, it is. But I am thankful for Canada."

"Are you going to play on the team?"

Sarimah's heart skipped a beat. "That would be nice. But I have never played on a team before. Maybe I am not ready."

Many of the parents laughed.

"You sure have us fooled, then," Lisa's mom said.

Sarimah was confused at first, but then it dawned on her. The parents thought she was a good player. She held her head high as they left for home — with plenty of time to spare.

★★★

Sarimah was helping her father with his English homework when someone knocked on the door. Even though Izzy's parents sometimes checked in on them, it was later than they normally visited. As her parents traded glances, Sarimah thought about how a knock on the door in Syria could be a dangerous thing.

Sarimah was surprised when her father answered the door to find Coach K. Sarimah wondered if she had done something wrong at the soccer practice. But her worry turned to excitement when Coach K invited her to play with the Blizzard.

With Sarimah translating, Coach K did his best to explain to her father.

"You have a very talented daughter," the coach told Sarimah's father. "But I probably don't have to tell you that. Someone taught her. I'm guessing it was you."

Sarimah translated for her father.

When her father responded, Coach K smiled. "Tell your father you didn't make up that part," he said.

"Tell him his flattery will not always work this well," Sarimah's father told her in Arabic.

"Does that mean I can play?" she asked.

"Yes, yes. I never wanted to stop you. I just wanted you to know what was most important: family and school."

"I will never forget, Papa. Thank you!"

14 UP FOR A CHALLENGE

Sarimah had played rough soccer before, but never against other girls. Usually, the boys knocked her over. She always tried to give some lumps back to them. She dipped her shoulder when going in for tackles. She slid for the ball. She kept her elbows out during corner kicks.

Sometimes it worked. But mostly she was just too small.

It was a good thing she had practised that, though, because she needed it now.

"Come on, girls," Coach K shouted as the girls went through their drills. "We play for the city championship next weekend. Dig deep!"

The coach tossed out the red pinnies. Sarimah didn't get one this time.

"I'll make corner kicks. Red team attacks and the rest of you defend," the coach told them.

He gathered up all the soccer balls and took them to one corner. He lined one ball up and curled it into the goal area. It landed a few yards in front of Sarimah, who had been battling against Giorgianna. Tamsen charged for it, and just got her head to it. It glanced off her forehead and out of bounds.

Coach K didn't wait before sending in the next one. Sarimah steadied herself and lined up closely against Giorgianna. The coach took a long run to the ball. He connected and the ball bent right for Sarimah and Georgianna. Sarimah sprinted toward it and jumped. It skimmed just over her. A player from the red team connected with it. It banged low toward Marty, who jumped to her left.

"Nice save, 'keeper," Izzy said, cheering. "Come on, Sarimah, let's see you climb the ladder."

It continued like that for another five minutes. Sarimah watched one ball after another soar overhead, or crash right in front of her. Her knee throbbed from diving for a kick that zipped across the goal, but she didn't get anywhere close to hitting it.

The teams traded places, and then it was Sarimah's turn to go for a goal. She was excited about getting the chance. The first corner kick was nearly perfect. It came, at the perfect speed, right to Sarimah's head. She pushed as hard as she could into the turf and did all she could to keep her eyes open.

It worked and she met the ball head-on, but it curled well wide.

"Your shoulders are facing the wrong direction, Sarimah. But that was a good try," the coach said.

"Okay, my legs are sore. Sarimah, why don't you take some kicks?"

"What? Why her?" Tamsen asked.

"Well, she's not going to out-jump many people," the coach said.

Not even Tamsen's complaining could ruin Sarimah's excitement. She had been hoping for a chance to kick the ball. Sarimah trotted to the corner and gathered up six soccer balls from around the sidelines.

Her first kick was a little low, but one player got a foot to it. It skipped just past the post.

"I am too tense," Sarimah said to herself.

She shook her legs out and placed another ball on the corner. This time, she let out a long breath. Her approach was better this time and she connected crisply. The ball rocketed off her foot and curled tightly toward the near post. Marty immediately scrambled.

"'Keeper's ball! 'Keeper's ball!" she screamed.

But Marty didn't get to it. Giorgianna knifed in front of her and flicked it into the top corner of the net. Coach K jumped into the air and started shouting.

"Yeah! That ball was exactly where we want it," he said. "Now try for the far post, Sarimah."

Sarimah set another ball on the ground. She took two steps back and paused, thinking about where to send the ball. She let out another breath and started her run. She powered her right foot through the ball, sending it high into the air. This time, the ball floated over Marty's head.

Waiting all alone at the back corner of the penalty area was Tamsen. She squared her shoulders to the ball and lunged. The ball sliced into the top corner of the net for another easy goal.

"Yes!" Coach K cheered. "I could watch that all day long. This is going to be just what we need in the tournament."

Sarimah spent the next five minutes placing the ball into the goal area. She perfected her approach so well, she felt like she could place it wherever the coach asked her.

"Okay," the coach said. "Now for some set pieces. Let's set up free kicks from outside the eighteen-yard box."

The players milled about. The defenders set up a wall. Sarimah gathered up some soccer balls. She followed the coach to a spot on the field about twenty yards from the goal. Tamsen and Kaelynn went there, too.

"You did good with the corners," Tamsen said to Sarimah. "But we have set plays for this."

"Tamsen, you looked pretty good in there with the headers," Coach K said. "Why don't you get back in there? And Kaelynn, if we have two players behind the ball, that's one fewer to go for a header. Let's let Sarimah try this."

The two girls stared at their coach. Sarimah shifted on her feet. The coach started placing the soccer balls on the turf. He looked up and spotted Tamsen still standing there, watching him.

"Coach, Kaelynn and I always take the free kicks," Tamsen said.

"Why is she getting all this special treatment?" Kaelynn added, looking at Sarimah. "Tamsen is our best player. She has been for a really long time."

The coach placed the last ball on the turf and turned toward the three girls. "First, I'm the coach. It's not for you to question my decisions," he said, counting on his fingers. "Second, Tammy, you know your knee isn't 100 per cent. Too many kicks will not help it. Third, Kaelynn, putting two people on the ball means we have one less to try for a header. Now, get going."

"This isn't fair," Tamsen said. "She is on our team without trying out and getting picked. And she's getting all the best chances."

The coach shook his head and placed his hands on his hips. "Tamsen, Kaelynn, you've both been great for this team. But now isn't the time for this. Get in there and score a goal. That's what we will need this weekend. So, that's what I need to see you practise now."

Sarimah felt like she was spying on them, but she couldn't leave. She didn't want to leave, either. She was having too much fun. All she could think of was putting the best passes to her teammates.

Maybe that will make everyone happier, she thought.

15 PLAYOFF TIME

Parents from both teams lined the concourse above the field. Still more filled a small set of bleachers on the sideline. They whistled and cheered. They clapped and waved pompoms. It was noisy.

Coach K called the girls to the sideline. Sarimah couldn't hear anything because of all the cheering. Her teammates formed a huddle. They swayed back and forth. Some tightened their laces, while others adjusted the elastics holding back their hair or pulled at their socks waiting for the coach to finish writing his notes on a clipboard. It was hard to breathe the hot, heavy air inside the Soccer Centre. Sarimah had never seen so many people inside the Soccer Centre before.

Coach K finally looked up at the team. "This is a short playoff series," he said, raising his voice.

Sarimah had to lean in to hear him over the whistles and clapping.

"We play just three games. We can move on to the finals with two wins. Let's show the other team we will set the pace. Never stop hustling!"

The girls clapped and each put a hand in the middle.

"Blizzard on three!" Izzy shouted. "One-two-three . . ."

The players shouted back: "Blizzard!"

Sarimah studied her teammates before the opening whistle. Tamsen had her eyes closed and Izzy was staring straight down. Giorgianna was jumping up and down, frowning and puffing out her cheeks.

Everyone looked serious. Then Sarimah glanced back at the other team. The Monarchs had gathered in small groups, while the referee talked to his assistants. The players were laughing and jumping around. Even when the referee finally blew the whistle to begin the game, they had big smiles on their faces.

Sarimah turned to Molly, who was sitting next to her on the bench. "Why do they look so happy?"

"Who? The parents?"

"No, the girls on the other team."

"I don't know. But you're right. They look really happy."

Soon, Sarimah felt that her teammates needed to relax, too. They started the game by running into their opponents, giving up silly fouls. They ran into each other, too. They were at odds with each other and trying to do too much.

After ten minutes, Tamsen finally found herself with space in the middle of the pitch. Instead of sending it wide to a winger, she tried to run with the ball. Two Monarchs converged on her and stripped her of the ball. They turned and headed in the other direction. The taller girl kicked the ball to the wing, where her teammate managed to gain valuable ground against the Blizzard.

"Keep her there!" Marty shouted from the goal. "No crosses!"

The warning didn't work. The Monarchs wiggled their way through the Blizzard's defence. The cross came at a good pace. Marty jumped from her line and tried to grab the ball from mid-air. But it was moving quickly and Marty couldn't hang onto it. She fumbled the ball and it bounced dangerously in her penalty area. Three Monarchs crowded around, looking to get a shot on goal. The Blizzard defence was too slow.

Marty was too far out of position and had no chance. Any of the three Monarchs could have scored. It was the tall girl everyone called Raimy who blasted it into the far corner.

"Yeah!" she shouted.

Sarimah looked up into the crowd and waved to her parents. They were sitting with Izzy's family. Her mom waved back with both hands and Sarimah laughed. At least they looked like they were having fun.

Sarimah noticed the Monarchs still looked happy, too. Then she looked at her teammates on the Blizzard. They still looked serious — almost angry. Tamsen tapped the ball ahead to Giorgianna. Then she took a big stride into the Monarchs' side of the field. "Yeah, here! Now!" Tamsen shouted. Sarimah knew what her teammate was doing. She was trying to force the play.

"Come back! Regroup," Sarimah said.

"Where's Tamsen going?" asked Molly. "Why is she trying to do everything by herself?"

Giorgianna still had the ball. She hesitated.

Tamsen clearly wasn't impressed. "Quick! Now!" she said, ordering Giorgianna to pass it to her.

Giorgianna finally sent the ball forward. Tamsen collected the pass with her back to the Monarch goal. Then she turned quickly, straight into two defenders who were clogging the middle of the field. Tamsen tried to cut hard to her right to get away from the defenders.

Instead of moving around the defenders, Tamsen suddenly crumpled in a heap. She screamed in pain, grabbing at her knee.

The Monarchs kicked the ball out of bounds so Tamsen could get some help. Coach K ran to the centre circle to check on the girl.

Sarimah walked forward. Tamsen was lying on the turf with Coach K and the referee on either side of her. Tamsen was holding her knee, her eyes closed tightly. Sarimah could see her chest going up and down as she cried.

Even the Monarchs' coach came onto the field to help. The coaches and the ref spent a few minutes asking Tamsen questions, but she just cried and shook her head. Finally, the coaches helped her to her feet. She tried to take a step, and nearly fell again. They hoisted her up and carried her off the field. Everyone on both teams clapped and Tamsen's parents met her at the sideline. Tamsen hugged her mother.

Izzy called the Blizzard into another huddle on the field. They watched as Tamsen's father carried the girl to the dressing room.

"We're one player down," Izzy said. "Tammy is a great player, one of our best. But each of you can play great, too. Let's show her how much she means to us, by winning this game! Tammy on three! One-two-three . . ."

The girls all shouted "Tammy!" and got back into position.

16 SOCCER SHOULD BE FUN

Sarimah decided she was not going to worry about Tamsen. She wasn't going to worry about scoring goals or winning the game. All she knew was that she wasn't having much fun. And that needed to change.

Sarimah charged back into her end to support Izzy. She thought that being next to her best friend might help her start enjoying the game.

As she arrived, the Monarchs tried to pass the ball through the centre of the field. Sarimah and Izzy shuffled close to each other and cut off the lane. The Monarchs had to turn back and start again.

This time, Lisa was able to pressure the ball along the Blizzard's left wing. She caught one of the Monarchs, but her back was facing her teammates and she had no one to pass to. Lisa stood guard and waited for help.

Sarimah realized what was happening and raced over to help her teammate.

The Monarchs' player tried to kick the ball back to her goalie, but Sarimah blocked it. The ball bounced off Sarimah's foot and skidded into the Monarchs' side.

Sarimah began to chase it, with one Monarch behind her and one waiting for her near the goal area. She took one touch of the ball to control it, and then kicked it softly into the centre of the field. The Monarchs looked around in shock. Why had she kicked the ball into empty space?

That's when Lisa — who had been following the play — pounced on the loose ball like a cat. She took two dribbles and let a shot go that sailed right for the far goal post. Sarimah watched the ball go flying. Silently, she urged it into the net.

Lisa's shot forced the Monarchs' goalie into a stretching, diving save. She managed to stop the ball and fall on top of it. Lisa and Sarimah charged the net, looking for a rebound. But the goalie held onto the ball.

"Great pass, Sarimah," Lisa said as they ran back into position. "How did you know I was going to be there?"

Sarimah just smiled and shrugged her shoulders. The Blizzard regrouped as the Monarchs' goalie kicked the ball into play. Sarimah was huffing and puffing from the hard play, but she was smiling. She looked around at her teammates, hoping to see more smiling faces. Instead, Izzy, Lisa and most of the others scowled back at her. Marty was yelling instructions from the goal as the first half ended.

The Blizzard was trailing 1-0. But for the first time in the game, they had controlled much of the play.

"That's better," Coach K said as they rested on the sideline for half-time. "Keep the pressure up and the goals will come. Just don't forget about Marty in our net."

The referee blew his whistle and signalled the girls to the field. Coach K moved Molly beside Sarimah and dropped Izzy into sweeper.

"We need to get some chances on goal," Coach K said, in the huddle. "Molly, use your speed. Sarimah can put the pressure on. Izzy is there to back you up. Don't forget about Kaelynn. You need to get the forwards more involved."

The girls took their positions. Sarimah looked at her teammates. They all seemed even more nervous now that Tamsen was out of the game. Sarimah walked over to Molly and raised her hand high in the air. "Syrian high-five," she said.

Molly slapped Sarimah's hand for a high-five. Then Sarimah signalled to Izzy, and her friend came running up for slap-hands with her. The same went for Rosy, Lisa and Giorgianna. As Sarimah connected with each girl, their smiles got a little bigger. By the time she had traded high-fives with all the girls around her, the whole team was laughing.

The team clapped and shouted encouraging words.

Marty, in goal, let out a holler, "Whoo-hoo!"

The Blizzard parents chimed in, too, adding to the noise in the Soccer Centre. It was so loud, it was hard to hear the referee's whistle to restart the game.

Rosy threw the ball back into play. She tossed it to the Monarch defender who had kicked it out of bounds so Tamsen could get help for her injury. The defender knocked the ball across the field. Giorgianna gave chase and Sarimah followed. The Monarch defender saw Sarimah lurking and cleared the ball down the field.

Izzy controlled the ball and the Blizzard sprang into action. Three girls cut hard toward Izzy, calling for a pass. She gave it to Lisa as Molly came in to support her.

That led to Sarimah finding space along the centre line. The ball went quickly to Kaelynn, Rosy and then Giorgianna. The Blizzard had gone from deep in their own end to the Monarchs' side of the field in just a few seconds.

"Beautiful!" the coach yelled from the sideline.

Sarimah heard him and her smile got bigger. The girls were finally having fun on the field.

The change in mood made soccer easy. The Blizzard kept possession, most of the second half, with Georgianna scoring ten minutes after the restart. Izzy and Sarimah made the difference. They supported the defence and fed the offence through Giorgianna.

With only five minutes left to play, Georgianna one-timed a low pass and beat the goalie on a breakaway to break the tie. When the final whistle sounded, the Blizzard had won! Sarimah felt like she could have kept running for days.

Tamsen had come back to the sideline. She was sitting with a bag of ice on her knee and red eyes from crying. Everyone gathered around her for a group hug.

"Be gentle, please," Tamsen said.

"Ugh," Kaelynn said. "Can you play the next game?"

Tamsen shook her head, "No. My knee is pretty sore. I might be done until summer and outdoor soccer."

They returned to the dressing room and sat on the benches. It was quiet when Coach K appeared with the schedule. "All right," he said to the team. "We play in the semi-finals later today against the Rebelles. They'll be good, so get something to eat. And remember to hydrate. It's warm in here."

Sarimah grabbed a bottle and squeezed a jet of ice water into her mouth. "It feels like the desert," Sarimah said to Izzy and Molly.

"But there's no sand," Molly said with a smile.

"Or camels," Izzy added. Then she stopped and a panicked look crossed her face.

Sarimah looked at Izzy, who appeared frozen with fear.

"I'm sorry," Izzy said. "Was that rude? I don't even know."

She scrunched up her shoulders as if she expected bad news, but Sarimah only laughed.

"It is okay," she said. "Aleppo had two million people before the war. I never spent much time in the country with any camels. I am a city girl."

It was Izzy's turn to laugh. "Oh, I feel so dumb," she said.

"It's cool that the city was so big," Molly said.

"It had many amazing things," Sarimah said. "Now, I am not so sure what is left."

Sarimah suddenly felt sad. She looked into the faces of her teammates. She saw they had stopped smiling, too.

"Let's not talk about that," she said. "We should be celebrating our win."

The girls were doing just that when a woman dressed in a black track suit appeared at the door. "Coach, can I have a word?" she asked Coach K.

Everyone watched as their coach and the woman shuffled away to speak privately. When Coach K returned, he didn't look happy.

"The other team is protesting," he said. "They claim we have an illegal player."

Sarimah wasn't sure what that meant, but the coach was staring right at her. Her smile disappeared.

17 UNLIKELY ALLY

"What do they mean, *illegal*?" Izzy asked. "We have had the same team since — well, since forever."

"Sarimah just joined us a little while ago," Coach K explained. "Their protest is about her." He looked concerned, but Sarimah could tell he wasn't angry with her. Everyone turned to look at Sarimah. It gave her the same feeling she had had at the first practice. She didn't like being the centre of attention on the sidelines. She preferred to get noticed by playing soccer on the field with her team.

"But she's not illegal," Molly said. "She came to Canada fair and square."

"That's not what they mean," Coach K said. "They mean she signed up too late, after the deadline."

The girls went silent. Sarimah's head started to spin.

"Is that true?" Izzy asked her coach. "Did she miss the deadline?"

"I don't think so. But I don't really know, to be honest," the coach said. "I signed her up on the last day and paid the fee. I didn't think to check. Nobody from the league office called me and nobody complained. Well, nobody complained until now."

"So, what are we supposed to do?" Izzy said.

"I have a meeting in ten minutes with the commissioner and the Monarchs' coach. Until then, prepare for the semi-finals."

The girls broke into smaller groups. Most grabbed their gym bags to change shoes. Sarimah could only watch them as they moved around her. A few of her teammates patted her shoulder.

"It's not your fault," Izzy said.

"We don't blame you," Molly added.

"We are going to win this," said Giorgianna.

Sarimah thanked them and nodded her head. When Izzy was alone changing her cleats, Sarimah saw her chance.

"What did I do?" she asked in a whisper.

"You didn't do anything. The other team thinks we cheated by having you on the team. But they just want us to be kicked out so they can play in the semi-finals."

Sarimah bent over to untie her cleats. She was fumbling with her laces when a shadow crossed over her. She looked up to see Tamsen, who had hobbled over. Tamsen leaned on the wall for support. She looked at Sarimah without saying a word.

"Someone help me," Tamsen finally said.

Kaelynn jumped up and Tamsen put her arm around her shoulders.

Sarimah watched as they limped away.

"Where are you going, Tammy?" Izzy shouted.

"To teach them the rules."

The team left the dressing room while they waited for the decision. Izzy and Sarimah had lunch together with their parents. Sarimah kept thinking about the meeting.

"Take it as a compliment," Izzy's mother told her. "The other team thinks you are too good."

It didn't help Sarimah to feel any better. She was worried sick about possibly costing the team its chance to move forward in the finals.

She didn't feel hungry for lunch.

"You must try to eat," her father told her. "You need your energy."

The girls returned to the field two hours later. The problem was, there were three teams on the field. There were the Rebelles, arch-rivals of the Blizzard. But the Monarchs were also there, hoping they would be the team to move on to play the Rebelles.

"There are a lot of players on this field," Sarimah said to Izzy.

"And one team is going to be very unhappy," she answered.

As the Blizzard girls waited at the bench, coaches from all three teams appeared together from the hallway.

They stopped just far enough away so that nobody could hear what they were saying. Tamsen walked in behind the coaches and moved past the group to her team.

"Hey, I told you to be ready."

The girls smiled and pulled up their socks, taped up their shin pads or tied their hair back. They didn't need to be told again to get set to play. They watched the Monarchs trundle off the field.

Coach K called the Blizzard into a huddle. "Tammy, you do the honours," he said.

Sarimah was standing near the back of the huddle. She leaned in to hear what the coach had said.

"Sarimah is part of our team," said Tamsen. "She joined us as an injury replacement, which is allowed under the rules."

Sarimah raised her head. What? This was the first she knew of an injury.

"Cool!" Rosy said. "I knew they were wrong."

Giorgianna moved closer to the centre. "But who was injured this year?" she asked.

"I was," Tamsen said. "I hurt my knee a month ago. I came back too early. It's been sore for a while."

Coach K stepped into the huddle again. "We looked at Sarimah's registration form. I submitted it on the deadline, but I just put the form into a mailbox. They didn't receive it or put it into the computer until the next day, the day after the deadline. It was my fault, but they didn't want Sarimah to pay for my mistake.

So, when Tamsen reminded them about the injury rule, they agreed that Sarimah deserves a place on our team."

The girls started to cheer and laugh. They clapped and patted each other on the back.

"Wow, way to go Tammy. You sure know a lot about the rules," Lisa said.

"My dad was commissioner for four years," Tamsen explained.

Sarimah turned away from the girls. She breathed out a big sigh of relief. Then she spotted her parents in the bleachers. She tried to smile, and then gave them a big thumbs-up. They clapped and waved.

Sarimah felt exhausted. And the game hadn't even started yet.

18 NEW STRATEGY

"What are *Rebelles*?" Sarimah asked as they warmed up for their next game.

"A rebel doesn't play by the rules," Izzy answered. "A *Rebelle* is a girl rebel, I guess. But it's not a real word. They just made it up."

Sarimah didn't like the name. It made her think about the war in Syria. "Why would they want that name?" she asked.

"I kind of like it," Tamsen said from the bench behind them. "What's wrong with it?"

"My uncle was helping the rebels in Syria," Sarimah said. "He would call us every day on his cell phone. One day, the phone went dead. We have not heard from him since."

The girls looked stunned.

"He was like a doctor," she added. "I can't remember the English word."

"A paramedic?" Tamsen asked.

"Medic! That's it. But he wanted to be a doctor

when he graduated from high school."

"High school? How old was he?" Izzy asked.

"He was sixteen when the war started. He is twenty-one now."

"My oldest brother is sixteen," Tamsen said. "He wants to be a paramedic when he graduates. That's freaky. I've decided I don't like the name any more, either."

Sarimah saw that everything was getting serious again. She wanted to change the mood back to excited and happy. "My uncle is clever. We are sure he is safe. Now, we have a game to win."

As Sarimah and Izzy started running drills to loosen up their muscles, Sarimah watched the other team.

"This team — they will be trouble," she told Molly and Giorgianna as the referee did his final preparations.

"Why do you say that?" Giorgianna asked her.

"I have a bad feeling. They look angry."

"They do look angry," Molly said. "I don't recognize any of them. Look at that tall girl. She looks extra angry."

The three girls stopped their drills and stood shoulder to shoulder to shoulder. The Rebelles were practising corner kicks. Sarimah watched as they banged and crashed against each other.

"They're going to be too injured to play by the time we start," Izzy said. She was watching the other team, too.

"I hope you are right," Sarimah said.

Once the game started, the Rebelles pressured the Blizzard at every turn. When Izzy had the ball in defence, she had no time to react. She had to kick it as far as she could. If she couldn't clear it, she would kick it out of bounds so the team could regroup.

Every time Sarimah looked up, she saw two Rebelles defending her. The pressure kept Lisa and Rosy on the wings. The Blizzard hardly touched the ball in the first half. The only time they were able to get a pass was after a free kick. The Rebelles were not afraid to knock the Blizzard players off their feet, even if it meant a foul.

It didn't turn into goals for either team, though. The first half ended scoreless.

"Why does it feel like they have twice as many players as we do?" Giorgianna said.

"It means someone is open," Sarimah said.

She looked around as the other players gathered to listen.

"If there are two of them on one of us, one of us must be unguarded. Look back instead of ahead. That is usually the easiest pass. My father always says it when he watches football."

Sarimah put on a serious face. She waved her finger in the air like an angry schoolteacher. "Sometimes you have to go backward to get ahead," she said in her father's deep voice.

All the girls laughed.

"I think he's right, you know," Tamsen said.

They stopped laughing and turned. Sarimah was worried Tamsen was going to get mad at them for laughing. But Tamsen was smiling.

"It's a good idea. Make them chase us," she said. "They look nervous. I don't think they know what to do when they don't have the ball."

"That makes sense," Kaelynn said. "When they have the ball, that big defender beside me just stops. She hardly moves. But when we get it, she starts running like my dog chasing a ball."

There were a few more laughs as the girls talked strategy. Sarimah listened, but didn't say much.

The Blizzard went into the second half with their new plan. Giorgianna started by tapping the ball ahead to Kaelynn. Kaelynn passed it back to Rosy, who pushed the ball all the way back to defence.

It went through the right side of the Blizzard team before the girls passed it ahead along the left. Sarimah could see the plan was working. The Rebelles chased the ball, but could not catch up to it.

Lisa received a pass about eight minutes into the second half. She had plenty of time and space on the left wing. She charged ahead, deep into the Rebelles' zone before crossing a beautiful pass into the goal area.

It was there that Kaelynn met the pass with a smashing header. It went straight down at the goalie's right side, deflected off the post and spun across the line. Kaelynn jumped and raised her fist.

The Rebelles never recovered. The 1-0 Blizzard win advanced them to the final game.

Everyone gathered at centre field to celebrate. They were laughing and clapping. Sarimah was right in the middle of the huddle. She felt like she was in a giant group hug.

19 FINAL FRIENDS

Sarimah and Izzy arrived at the Soccer Centre forty-five minutes before the final game. Sarimah showed her parents around the building. They looked at the different team photos on the walls.

"So many teams are just girls," her mother said. "That is so nice."

Sarimah hugged both her parents when they found a seat in the bleachers. She walked to the dressing room to find she was the first one there. She grabbed her shoes from her backpack. She wasn't alone for long before the door opened again.

"How's it going?" Tamsen asked.

"Good, thank you. How is it going for you?"

Tamsen lowered herself gently to the bench. Sarimah studied the brace on Tamsen's knee. It was a deep red and surrounded her leg in metal, plastic, and foam. Velcro straps circled her knee.

"It looks bad," Sarimah said.

"I'll be fine. As long as I'm ready for outdoor

soccer. That's more important."

Sarimah nodded. "Yes, I can hardly wait for the sunshine."

Sarimah wasn't sure why Tamsen was talking to her after weeks of ignoring or insulting her.

They sat in silence for what felt like forever. Tamsen finally shifted in her seat again and started to talk.

"Look, I'm bad at this. But I want to tell you I'm sorry. I got mad at you at school when I hurt my knee. But, really, I was mad at myself because it was still sore when I had told everyone it was better. I rushed back into playing. It wasn't your fault."

Sarimah was trying to stay calm, but she wanted to yell and scream. She was mad at Tamsen for putting her through so much trouble. But she knew it wasn't easy for Tamsen to apologize to her.

She decided to stay calm.

"Thank you," Sarimah said. "I know how it feels when you want to play so badly but you cannot."

"I guess refugee camps aren't the best places for soccer," Tamsen said.

"We were lucky. We left Syria earlier than a lot of others did, as soon as the fighting started. We lived in a camp. It was better than most. But it was different. There was no home to go to, after."

Tamsen stretched her leg a little. There was another pause.

"Did you play much in Syria?" Tamsen asked.

"I would play whenever I could; in the street or in the park. There were many children where I lived."

"You must have been on a good team. I mean, you are so good," Tamsen said.

"Well, I feel like I don't know much, compared to you. But I learned a lot from my father. He loves to watch. He used to play a lot, too," Sarimah said.

"But you probably never played in the snow before."

"No, that is new for me. I am still having trouble with it."

"Nobody is very good in the snow. It's just for fun. You really try hard, though. And you made the team happy to play and to have fun again. I like that. Anyway, I'll let you get ready. Good luck."

While Sarimah and Tamsen were talking, the rest of the team arrived. They were quiet, as they changed for the game.

Sarimah was eager to play. As she ran onto the field, she felt like she was leaping through the air. She finally felt like she belonged on the team.

Coach K called them all together. "Okay, we are playing the Sparks," he said. "We know what to expect from them. They play smart, but there won't be anything flashy. Play your game, and we should be just fine."

He barked out some final orders and the girls charged through their warm-ups.

"We finally made it to the finals," Izzy said, as they

huddled for a pre-game cheer. "Let's just keep playing the way we did in the semis."

"Make it fun. Don't forget that part," Tamsen said.

Izzy looked surprised that the advice was coming from Tamsen. Then she laughed. Sarimah smiled at Tamsen. She looked around to see her teammates giggling in the huddle.

Finally, Sarimah thought. *Everyone is happy.*

The Blizzard stormed their opponents right from the start of the game. Giorgianna stripped the ball from a defender five minutes in. She passed it back to Kaelynn near the centre dot. Kaelynn kicked it all the way back to Izzy. From there, it went to Rosy, back to Sarimah and over to Lisa. The Sparks could only watch.

Every time a Sparks player tried to pressure the Blizzard, they moved the ball. Eventually, the Sparks retreated. They formed a defensive shell just outside their eighteen-yard box.

The Blizzard moved ahead easily. But they had to shoot from far away because of the tough defence. Few of their shots got close enough to threaten the Sparks' goalie.

Sarimah and her teammates weren't smiling as the first half ended.

"Don't worry so much about the time," Coach K said, during the break. "The chances will come. The Sparks know they can't catch us."

Sarimah grabbed a water bottle and took a drink and then handed the bottle to Molly. Sarimah saw someone coming toward her.

"Papa?"

The other girls looked at Sarimah, and then at her father. He was standing just outside the field. Coach K walked over to him and smiled.

"Welcome," he said. "It is wonderful to see you again."

Sarimah ran to give her father a hug. He shook hands with Coach K and then wrapped an arm around his daughter's shoulders.

"What are you doing here?" she asked him.

"I do not wish to interrupt. I love football," he said in halting English. "I have a plan."

"We're happy for the help. Let's hear it," Coach K said.

Sarimah's father spoke to Sarimah in Arabic.

"It's too complicated for his English," she told the coach. "I'll translate."

"He says we need to crowd the right side," Sarimah explained. "That is where the defence is weak. Overlap and look for a pass into their area. But not just in the air. We should go along the ground and sometimes behind the play, back to the top of the box."

Sarimah knew her father liked soccer and knew a lot about it. But she had never heard him speak with such authority. He sounded just like a real coach. She tried to sound the same way.

"I was thinking the same thing. Let's try it," said Coach K. He grinned. "And maybe your father should come to more practices and games."

Sarimah hugged her father again before he returned to his seat. Sarimah had never been more proud of him.

20 NAME GAME

Coach K called the Blizzard into a huddle. He told the girls what to try in the second half. Most of it was what Sarimah's father had said.

Within minutes, the girls had found a way down the right side.

Sarimah and Rosy controlled the ball along the wing. Each girl kicked a crossing pass right at the goalie. Giorgianna was there to go for the passes.

Coach K urged Kaelynn and Molly to join the rush to help her. Suddenly the Blizzard's players were able to find some open space in the penalty area.

Rosy crossed two passes in a row. But the Blizzard couldn't get headers on goal. Lisa tried a pass along the turf from the other side. Molly was there to one-time it, and her shot forced the goalie to dive across her net.

Sarimah thought that Molly was going to score for sure. But she watched as the goalie made another great save. Even so, the Blizzard was getting somewhere with the new strategy.

At least the smiles have started to appear again, thought Sarimah.

Sarimah and Izzy continued to chase down everything in the middle of the park. Lisa and Rosy ran up and down the sidelines, getting more chances to cross the ball into the goal area.

The Sparks' goalie was tall and fast. Until now, the Blizzard players hadn't really tested her. When they did, they found that she was up to the challenge.

Sarimah was starting to get nervous. She thought the game must be nearly over. The smiles and the energy on her team were fading. And the Sparks were starting to take more chances.

It was still 0–0. Sarimah decided she needed to take a chance.

Rosy was battling a defender on the right wing. Rather than join her, Sarimah sprinted to the centre of the field. The Sparks player didn't see her and tried a pass back to her goalie. Sarimah was there to intercept the ball in the penalty area. She stopped it, dragged it back a little and looked for an opening.

Before she could shoot or pass, a defender knocked her down from behind.

"Oof!"

Tweeeeet!

Everyone on the Blizzard side jumped and cheered. Sarimah looked up in time to see the referee pointing to the penalty spot.

The Sparks shouted in protest.

"My player was going for the ball!" screamed the Sparks' coach from the sideline. "It was fifty-fifty! The Blizzard player is so tiny! She falls so easily!"

The ref didn't even look at the Sparks' bench. He just motioned everyone away from the penalty spot and called Sarimah to the dot. He handed her the ball and walked back to the goal line.

Sarimah held the ball in her hands. It was spongy, yet firm. The Soccer Centre's lights reflected off its surface. She looked around. Everyone was staring at her, players and fans alike.

Sarimah decided it was okay to be centre of attention this time. She was on the field, playing a game. That made it all right for people to stare at her. Besides, the last time she took a penalty shot she had been wearing snow boots. The time before that, she had been in a refugee camp with Hassan and Aamir. She couldn't believe how much had changed in such a short time.

She could only hope her friends from the camp were as happy as she was now. She hoped they had been able to find somewhere better to live.

"This is for Hassan and Aamir," she said to herself.

Sarimah put the ball down and stepped back. She looked at the bottom-right corner of the goal before starting her approach. Sarimah studied the same right-hand side until she noticed the goalie's eyes glance in that direction. The goalie shuffled a little to that side.

That was what Sarimah was hoping to see. She started her run, picking up a little extra speed at the end. She raised her right foot and swung hard. She used the side of her foot to keep the ball low.

Instead of shooting for the right, though, she hit the ball hard to her left. The goalie fell for the fake and jumped in the opposite direction.

Sarimah scored into the open side of the net.

★★★

After the celebrations following the game, and once the Blizzard players accepted their gold medals, Sarimah found herself sitting alone.

She had hugged everyone on her team twice. Coach K came over to shake her hand. "I want to talk to your father," the coach said. "I think I have a job for him."

Sarimah watched the two men talk, off to one side. She put her soccer cleats into her bag and stood up to join her father.

"You had better keep those boots somewhere safe," someone said.

Sarimah turned to see Izzy standing alone, behind her.

"Well, I will be able to use them in the future," Sarimah said with a smile. "They are a little too big, still."

Izzy laughed.

"Hey, that was a great game," Izzy said. "I am so glad you played with us this year."

Sarimah gathered her equipment. Together, the two friends walked slowly toward the exit.

"Did I ever tell you, I admire your name?" Sarimah asked. "*Isobel* is a very holy name."

Izzy stopped walking. She scrunched up her nose as she looked at Sarimah, but she didn't say anything.

"Don't you know what your name means? It means *pledged to God*. I looked it up in the library. Where I am from, what your name means is important."

"That's cool. Thanks. I've always gone by *Izzy*, after my grandmother, Elizabeth. Are you very religious?"

"Oh," Sarimah said. "It is important for most Muslim people, at least a little bit. For my family, it is important. But it's not all we think about. We like soccer, too."

"I think that's just like our family. What does *Sarimah* mean?"

"Well, it means many things, but mostly it means *brave*."

Izzy looked over at Sarimah as they reached the door that would lead them into the spectators' area.

"*Brave*, huh? That's awesome."

"Thank you. It could also mean *strong* or *courageous*, and *wise*, too."

Sarimah could see a smile start to spread across Izzy's face.

"Oh, sure. You're just fooling with me now, aren't you? It can't mean all those things."

"No, I am being honest," Sarimah said.

"I'm sorry," Izzy said, turning a little red. "Wow, that's an amazing name. But, you know what?"

"Yes?"

"It makes total sense. All those things you did, all that stuff you had to go through in Syria? That was so brave. Your name fits you perfectly."

Sarimah could feel her heart beating quickly. She had not been this happy since before the war started. She felt more at peace than she had in years. Being in Canada and playing soccer with her friends made her feel at home.

"You know," said Sarimah. "My name, it also means *beautiful*. And *smart*. And *really good at soccer*."

Izzy gave Sarimah a puzzled look. Then they both burst out laughing.

"You believed me, didn't you?" asked Sarimah.

"Not for a second," Izzy said, laughing. "But I believe you are going to do just fine here in Canada."

ACKNOWLEDGEMENTS

This book wouldn't have been possible without the thoughtful and thorough guidance of editor Kat Mototsune. To all the staff at Lorimer for their work in helping this book become reality, thank you. Special thanks to Alya Ramadan and her family for their insights. I'm grateful for early guidance from Project Literacy in Kelowna. Finally, this is for any girl who just wants the chance to play soccer.